ORLAND PARK PUBLIC LIBRARY
P9-EMP-914

THE VAMPIRE IN MY BATHTUB

THE VAMPIRE IN MY BATHTUB

Brenda Seabrooke

Holiday House/New York

Printed in the United States of America
FIRST EDITION

Library of Congress Cataloging-in-Publication Data
Seabrooke, Brenda.
The vampire in my bathtub / Brenda Seabrooke.—1st ed.
p. cm.
Summary: After moving into an old house, thirteen-year-old Jeff opens a locked closet and finds an ancient, good vampire named Eugene, who is being hunted by his cousin Louis, an evil vampire from New Orleans.
ISBN 0-8234-1505-8
[1. Vampires Fiction.] I. Title.
PZ7.S4376Vam 1999
[Fic]—dc21 99-19709
CIP

For K.C.
and K.D.

THE VAMPIRE IN MY BATHTUB

PROLOGUE

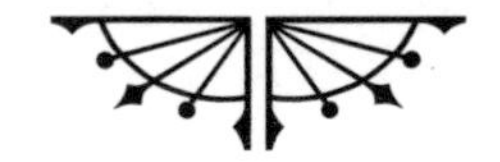

New Orleans: 12:01 A.M. CDT

Felix brings an envelope to a chubby man sitting at a table in a New Orleans restaurant. The man frowns as he reads his name on the envelope, Monsieur Eugene Carondelet. He breaks the dark red wax seal, like a drop of hardened blood on the thick paper. Carlotta wishes him to meet her. He hurries out and hails a cab. "The Cashbeau warehouse. Hurry."

Eugene enters the dark warehouse. The heavy door slams behind him. A voice whispers, "Here, Eugene, in this trunk. Come and join me. It is almost dawn."

He climbs in and falls asleep instantly. He does

not hear the snap of the trunk's lock. He does not hear fists pounding on the warehouse door and a woman's voice screaming, "Non, non, Eugene, it is a trick! Do not listen. Vennard sent the note." He does not feel the trunk as it is borne upward, nor its descent into the hold of a ship. He does not notice the motion of the paddle-wheeler as it battles the current in its journey northward. He sleeps deeply and peacefully.

CHAPTER 1

Wicklow, West Virginia: 3:03 P.M. EDT

For the hundredth time I twisted the doorknob of the closet door and yanked. My arm was almost wrenched out of its socket from previous attempts but I had to get it open. I'm thirteen. No door is going to get the best of me. I tried again.

Nothing.

The knob was just what every guy wants in his room—a white china doorknob with a circle of rosebuds painted around the edge, a doorknob that wouldn't turn on a door that wouldn't open.

The closet wasn't really a closet—not the kind I was used to in our old house in Washington, D.C. This one stuck out into my room on the left side of the door to the hall. There was another closet on the right side of the door. That one opened perfectly. It didn't have a lock. It didn't have rosebuds on its knob either. It had daisies. But it was crammed with clothes and sports equipment, and I needed a place to store my hubcap collection, my weights, my comic-book collection, my boomerang from Luray Caverns, games I don't play anymore but might sometime, the model kits I got when I had the flu and never finished putting together but might next time. You get the picture.

I slid a screwdriver into the crack.

"Jeff! Stop that!" Mom stood in the doorway holding a load of towels.

"I have to get the door open, Mom." She gave me a look. A mother look—the kind that goes all the way through you. I took the screwdriver out of the crack.

"You'll have to make do with the other closet. Don't shred the door. It's not our house, Jeff. We're only renting." She sighed. Mom wasn't happy about living in a rented house. But *she* was the one who had decided to come here, not me.

"I don't like having a locked closet around. What if there's a body in it?" I grinned fiendishly.

She ignored my grin and took the towels into the bathroom. "I think we'd know from the smell," she said with a laugh.

"It could be a skeleton. They found a skeleton in a boarded-up closet in a house in England. It was sitting in a chair. With a book in its lap. Probably trying to win the summer reading contest at the library." Mom was always telling me to read when I complained about having nothing to do. There really hadn't been a book in the skeleton's lap. I just put that in. But the rest of the story was true. The house was called Ightham Mote. I said it aloud. It had a sinister sound.

"Don't be morbid." She came into my room.

"There could be anything in that closet. It could be a zombie. Or a ghost. It could creep out at night . . ." I grabbed her shoulders.

She laughed again and went downstairs saying with that much imagination I should write a book. She turned on the computer to work on her class assignments. We'd been here a week already. Soon it would be the end of June. The summer was passing by.

I didn't want to write a book. I wanted to play ball with my friends, go swimming, haunt the mall, see some movies. But there was no pool, no mall, no movie theater. And I didn't have any friends. I didn't even have any enemies. Well, not real ones.

I couldn't even get hooked up to the Internet until school started. By then I'd be settled in. Mom didn't want me to turn into a Net freak. But this was when I really needed the connection, not in September.

We'd moved here after Mom got a job teaching fifth grade starting in the fall. "It's a new life," she said. I didn't want a new life. I wanted my old one. I didn't know anybody here. That wasn't hard. There was hardly anybody to know. Wicklow, West Virginia. Population—1,009.

Correction—1,011.

I kicked the closet door.

"A little less noise, please," Mom called up the stairs. "I can't concentrate with that earthquake up there."

I wanted to yell back, "So? I've had an earthquake in *my* life and I'm concentrating on this door," but didn't. It wasn't her fault. It wasn't my fault. It wasn't Dad's fault. These things just happen, they say.

I wanted it to be somebody's fault. I kicked the door again, but not as hard.

The room was hot and stuffy. The house wasn't air-conditioned. It didn't even have the giant ceiling fans our other house had. Just a little fan that turned its face from side to side as though it couldn't make up its mind.

"We don't need air-conditioning in West Virginia," Mom had said.

"Why? Don't they have summer there?" I'd asked.

She'd laughed. It seemed like she laughed at everything, especially everything I said now. "That's a good one. Of course they have summer there. Right after May and just before September. But the town is on the river and has giant trees that keep it cool. We won't need air-conditioning. You'll see."

And we hadn't. Until today. I had to get out before I broke something. "Going out, Mom," I called.

I stopped at the front door and opened it a crack to check the house next door. Coast clear. I jumped the porch steps and loped across the scruffy lawn. A clean getaway.

"Hey, Jefferson! Where's the fire?"

It was the girl next door. Bat Ears. She didn't really have bat ears. It's just that every time I try to leave the house, she's there asking questions. I swear she hears me before I open the front door. "Where're you going? What're you doing? Want to come over?" Even when I tiptoe out of the house, she hears me. She can probably hear the grass growing.

Mom thinks it's great that there's a built-in best friend right next door, but I don't want a best friend in Wicklow, West Virginia. I want my own best friends, Billy Brown and Tommy Nguyen. I don't want some girl who shrieks every time she sees me and doesn't even get my name right.

"Jefferson! Jefferson!"

I never answer her. But it was pretty hard to ignore her this time because she was leaning out her upstairs window screeching, "Jefferson! Where are you going, Jefferson?" at the top of her voice.

I crossed the street and turned around. "Hey, Bat Ears. My name isn't Jefferson."

That shut her up. I'd never spoken to her before. She stared back at me and blushed. At least I think that's what she was doing. Maybe it was instant sunburn. Anyway her face turned almost as red as her hair. And then she disappeared.

Our street, Stephens Street, would have gone straight into the Tuscarora River if it hadn't forked first and changed its name to River Street. The right fork went into Wicklow. The left fork turned into a dirt road. I followed it along the river. The brown water slid smooth as a snake between the banks. I threw a rock at a sunken rowboat. A squadron of frogs hit the water.

If I had a boat, I could explore the river. A canoe or a kayak would be great. How much would they cost? I could save my allowance since there was nothing here to spend it on anyway.

This was really the pits. Dad had moved into a house in Georgetown. It had been Moira's house but now it was his, too, since they got married. It was old, but it had air-conditioning and a small room for me whenever I visit. The room was in the cellar next to the furnace and awfully small but it was mine, they said. I could keep some of my things there, they said. Moira and Dad. She's a lawyer, too. She got some posters from the zoo and hung them on the walls: pandas and white tigers and camels. Like I was a little kid.

I was supposed to spend the summer with them while Mom took classes in summer school, then move up here when school started. But it didn't happen that way. Dad and Moira got a big case and were working night and day. Practically living in the law library, they said. So I came here with Mom. "You'll make friends fast," Dad said. "I have confidence in you."

Yeah. Who's here to make friends with and why would I want to? Why couldn't Mom get a job in Washington? Why did she have to go so far away from Dad and my friends, and civilization? So far nobody had answered this for me. I kicked some rocks loose and threw them as hard as I could into the river. I walked a little farther but it all looked the same, so I turned around and jogged back to town.

Town was a hardware store, a gas station/convenience grocery store, two fossilized antique stores that nobody ever went into, a junk shop that four people a week went into, the Frizzeria (a pizza/burger/ice-cream place), a volunteer fire station, a post office, a dentist's office (the dentist came two days a week from Gistville forty-five miles away), three churches, Catholic, Episcopal, and Presbyterian (but they only had services twice a month), and a tiny bank. A part-time town.

I'd been in every store except the junk shop and one antique store, The Yesterday Shop. It had a permanent yellowed, fly-specked, out-to-lunch sign on the door. I hadn't tried the junk shop yet. The hands on the clock of the Episcopal church tower pointed to three o'clock. Time seemed to crawl by in Wicklow, West Virginia. I checked my watch—4:03. Nobody had even bothered to change the clock to daylight saving time. I went in the gas station grocery and bought an ice-cream bar.

I sank my teeth into the frozen chocolate. It made a snapping sound. There were no people on the street when I came out. My kind of town.

Correction.

There was one person on the street.

CHAPTER 2

Wicklow, West Virginia: 4:09 P.M. EDT

Bat Ears!

She bounced along in jean shorts and a green shirt, her red hair glowing in the sun. She hadn't seen me yet. I dropped the ice-cream bar and ducked behind a gas pump.

Then I slid into Collectibles & Other Valuable Junque. A bell tinkled over the door. The shop was dim and crammed with everything in the world: old books, umbrellas, dishes, walking sticks, glass pitchers, chairs, bottles, pottery, figurines, candlesticks, clocks, a you-name-it-we've-got-it sort of place. Everything except a canoe or kayak. I tripped over a battered green watering can, stubbed my toe on a small anchor, and almost fell into a wicker baby carriage with a stuffed mermaid and an almost furless monkey nestled inside.

"Help you?"

The man was short and rotund with a fringe of fluffy white hair around his shiny pink head. He looked at me over little half-moon glasses.

"I, um, was just looking." I grabbed a box of old postcards and thumbed through them. A red blur appeared through the window. I dropped a card and bent to retrieve it.

I stayed bent over, brushing off the card to give Bat Ears time to pass. My eyes focused on a glass jar, a quart mayonnaise jar. It was packed with keys. One of them might fit the door in my room.

"Um, how much for the jar?"

"Jar's free. Keys'll cost you."

Joke. Grown-ups.

"Okay. How much for the keys?"

The man squinted through his glasses. "How 'bout a dollar?"

I resisted saying, "How about it," and felt around in my pockets. Two coins clinked.

"But today I have a half-price special. For one day only keys are fifty cents a jar."

I pulled out the two quarters and put them on

the counter. He picked them up. "You the new boy moved into the Cashbeau house?"

I was probably the only new boy in town. Maybe the only old boy. I nodded. "I didn't know it was called that."

"Cashbeau family came up the river from New Orleans. Built that house in 1853."

I stared at him. "How did they do that?"

He looked at me over his glasses. "You don't know how people build houses?"

"No, how did they come upriver from New Orleans?"

"In a steamboat up the Mississippi, then up the Ohio, then up the Tuscarora. Wicklow was a port city then."

"Why would anybody leave New Orleans to come here?"

"People have all sorts of reasons for going places."

I could have stayed to chat all day but wanted to try the keys. By now Bat Ears must have gone wherever she was going.

She was in front of the out-to-lunch sign. "Aha! You can't get away this time!" She grinned. The sun hit her braces. The effect was blinding.

She had followed me, made me drop my ice-cream bar, lurked outside waiting for me, and now was gloating about it.

"Oh, yeah? Well, watch this, Bat Ears." I sprinted down River Street.

A second later I heard footsteps behind me. I wasn't worried—I'd been running since I learned to walk. I made the jog around the cemetery, then headed up Stephens Street. The footsteps disappeared somewhere near the jog. I slowed to a walk.

Stephens Street was really steep here, good for sledding in winter, but not for running up on a hot summer day.

She wasn't behind me. The hill was probably too much for her. I'd showed her.

Wrong.

"What are you doing with those keys?"

She stepped from behind the lilac bushes between our houses. She grinned, not even out of breath.

"How'd you do that?"

"My secret."

Her eyes were the color of her shirt. They looked like frogs might jump out of them as she gloated. Obviously she had a shortcut somewhere.

"What are those keys for?"

Now it was my turn to grin. "My secret, Bat Ears."

"Why do you call me that? My ears don't stick out." She put her hands up to check.

"My secret," I repeated.

"Alison!" A woman came out of the house next door. Probably her mother. I bypassed the steps and hit the porch running. Safe.

Wicklow, West Virginia: 4:47 P.M. EDT

I didn't stop until I was in my room. I dumped the keys on my bed and picked up a long, old-fashioned one with a fancy design on the head.

"Jeffrey!" Mom's voice came up the stairs. "Jeffrey, come down please. We have company." It was our next-door neighbor, Mrs. Gennero. And Bat Ears, alias Alison Gennero. They had brought a rectangle of lemon bread wrapped in plastic on a flowered paper plate. Appetizing.

"I was away earlier this week and now I'm behind in everything," Mrs. Gennero's voice trailed off in a laugh as she apologized for not coming over sooner to welcome us.

I thought they'd never leave. Bat Ears showed

her braces. Mrs. Gennero talked about Wicklow, what a lovely town it was for raising children, so safe, no crime.

"Why, we don't even have a policeman!" she said. Her hair was almost the same color as Bat Ears', only a little darker. They looked a lot alike, too. But Mrs. Gennero didn't have braces and her eyes were a warm, friendly brown. She had two little kids away visiting their grandmother. Mr. Gennero was an engineer and commuted to jobs around the state. "We'll be happy to have Jeff stay with us at night when you're in class," she said when they finally got up to leave. "Just send him over."

"Oh, what an enormous relief," Mom gushed. "It was so boring for him to have to tag along with me. I'm sure he will enjoy being with Alison."

I tried to glower at Mom and smile politely at Mrs. Gennero at the same time. It was hard.

Correction.

Impossible.

Mom gave me a look, but she didn't say anything. After they left I helped with supper because she had to finish typing a paper. I ate slowly and was only halfway through when she looked at the clock.

"Oh no! Look at the time." She grabbed her book bag and started out the door. "Go to the Genneros' when you finish your supper," she flung over her shoulder, "and remember to lock the door after you."

"Ummmm," I said.

The phone rang while I was rinsing my dishes. It was Bat Ears. "Mom said to come on OVER," she said emphatically.

"I have some things to do," I said. "Maybe some other time."

"Your mother SAID—"

"My mother left me HERE," I said. Two could play at that game. I hung up while she was telling me what to do.

Wicklow, West Virginia: 7:31 P.M. EDT

The keys were spread all over my bed. There must have been a hundred, all sizes and shapes. I inserted the long fancy key in the lock. It turned but the door didn't budge.

I tried another. And another. I went through the whole jar of keys. It seemed to take forever. Then I started over, but none of the keys would move the lock except the long one. I turned it and heard a click. Nothing. I examined the key. It seemed older than the others. It was also the fanciest.

I tried the key once more. This time I turned it twice. The lock clicked both times but the door wouldn't open. I turned it a third time.

And then without my even touching the knob, the door slowly swung open with a mournful creak.

CHAPTER 3

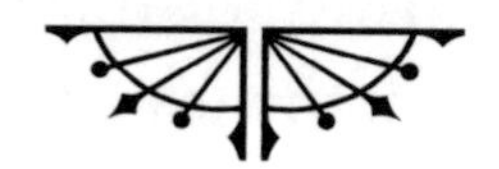

New Orleans: 6:37 P.M. CDT

The sleeper jerks suddenly but does not awaken. He lies under a velvet coverlet in an ornate bed. The room, silent except for the distant purr of the air-conditioning, is as dark as a tomb. The sleeper tosses restlessly, twisting the sheets. He mutters to himself. "Non, non, Eugene, you little maggot. You will not have Carlotta. You will not ruin my plans again with your stupid clumsiness."

Wicklow, West Virginia: 7:39 P.M. EDT

Light spilled into the closet. I jumped back. I don't know what I expected. The skeleton from

Ightham Mote. All the monsters from my childhood dreams. Bat Ears. Fanged spiders with crazed eyes hanging from their webs. I expected it to be empty or maybe filled with junk like old baby carriages, clothes smelling of mothballs, dollhouses, volleyball nets, stuff like that. But this closet was empty except for one thing. A trunk.

A *very* old trunk. Its curved lid was coated with at least an inch of dust and the lock was scrolled and secured with a fancy padlock. It had a design of leaves and acorns around the edge. It reminded me of something. I pawed through the keys on my bed until I found a small black one. It had the same design. But the acorns were not acorns at all. They were skulls. This was getting spooky.

Maybe I didn't want to open the trunk. I was alone in the house and suddenly shadows began to move with every creak of the boards. This was an old house. *A very old house*—1853 the man in the shop said.

Skulls were used to scare away treasure hunters. Maybe the Cashbeaus had been pirates. The trunk might be filled with pirate's treasure, gold and silver coins, emerald rings, ruby necklaces, diamond tiaras. We'd be rich. Mom wouldn't have to work. We could move back to Washington. Buy a house. A kayak. Go to Hawaii. I was getting excited.

But things happen to people who open up treasure troves. I'd seen those Indiana Jones videos. I got my baseball bat out just in case. Nothing alive could be in the trunk. Mom and I had lived in the house a week. The closet had been locked all that time. Nothing could live that long in a trunk . . .

I slid the key in the padlock and turned it. The lock sprang open and I raised the trunk lid. Something was in there. Something furry and big.

It was moving.

CHAPTER 4

New Orleans: 6:42 P.M. CDT

"Who is there?" the sleeper calls. His voice seems to come from the bottom of something very deep and dark. A well. "Eugene, is that you?"

Silence. Then he answers himself. "It cannot be. I made sure of that."

Wicklow, West Virginia: 7:43 P.M. EDT

What do you do when your worst nightmare comes true? You scream, right?

Wrong. I opened my mouth but no sound came out. If the thing in the trunk had been a bear, I'd be a goner. Ditto for a cobra. I just stood there with my mouth flapping, calling for my mom like some little kid, "MMM . . . mmmm . . . ," but I couldn't even get the word out. I was scared.

The thing kept unfolding. It had body parts. They were adding up. My frozen brain tried to put them together. But it didn't want to. I looked down and realized that I was holding my baseball bat. I gripped it and whacked at the thing.

The furry part was a head. Hands and arms reached up to protect it from the bat, which hit mostly the sides of the trunk.

"Mais non," it squeaked. "Non, non, non!"

The voice sounded human even if it was speaking French. I stopped hitting it, but kept the bat ready.

The thing stepped out of the trunk and backed away from me, its hands held out protectively.

I backed away from it in the opposite direction. We stared at each other, both of us breathing hard. After a while I said, "You—you're a man!"

"Mais oui. The trunk, it is so small, no? I have the cramp from how do you say, folding myself up?" He stretched.

"How—how did you get in there?" He was

bigger than I was, but I had the bat. I could leap across the bed if he came after me. I got ready.

But he only yawned and said, "I do not remember. When the dawn comes, I must sleep in a dark place. It must have been all that was available this morning. I assure you, it is not my habit to sleep in a trunk."

He stretched again and rubbed his back. He wasn't as tall as my dad but was several inches taller than me. His hair was dark brown, combed straight back from his face. His nose sloped way down and he had dark eyes that looked sleepy. He had a droopy brown mustache and long sideburns. I couldn't guess his age but I thought he was at least twenty-five. He wore an old-fashioned brown coat and trousers, a mustard-colored vest embroidered with olive green leaves and salmon-colored flowers, and funny shoes. They didn't seem to have a right or left.

"Who—who are you?"

"I am Eugene Aloysius Pierre Phillippe Carondelet, at your service." He made a funny little bow. "And whom do I have the honor of addressing?"

"Oh, I'm Jeff. Jeffrey Randolf Martin."

He made that little bow again.

I sort of made one, too. I guess it was catching.

"Why aren't you dead?" I blurted. Okay it's a rude question. But this man had been in my closet for a week without food or water or a bathroom. Without making noise.

"Dead?" His eyes were a little close together, making him look puzzled. I guess being locked up for a week in a trunk could make anybody puzzled.

"But I can't die," he said as though it were the worst thing in the world.

I raised the bat again and wondered if the drugs given to mental patients could cause them to live in a trunk for a week or longer.

"What is that stick?" He pointed at the bat.

"It's a bat."

"That is not a bat. A bat, it has wings and flies around at night."

"It's a baseball bat."

"What kind of bat is a baseball bat?"

He was a bagel brain. No question. "The kind you hit a ball with. Somebody throws a ball and I hit it. Like this." I swung at an imaginary ball.

He dodged.

"No, I wasn't swinging at you. It's a game."

"Oh, a game. I see. I do not know this game."

That explained it, I thought. He was a foreigner.

Wrong. "How long have you been in this country?"

"One hundred and seventeen years."

I stared at him. My ears weren't working right. I needed Bat Ears. He couldn't have said what I thought he said. "What did you say?"

"One hundred and seventeen years."

"Did you say you've been in this country for one hundred and seventeen years?"

"Exactement."

This was getting too weird for me.

Correction. This was already too weird for me. I should call the police. Then I remembered. Wicklow, West Virginia, doesn't have any police.

"Okay. Let's see if I've got this straight. You've been in the trunk a week, right?"

He gave a little shrug. "I do not know. This is what you say. It must be true."

"It's true. Okay. You've been in the trunk a week." I knew I was babbling but something inside me didn't really want to go on with this. "Okay. You've never heard of baseball. Right?"

He spread his hands and looked apologetic. "It sounds like a game of fun."

"It is." I still didn't believe him. Even people in other countries know about baseball. Some, like Japan, are fanatics about it. "Okay. And you've been in this country for, um, one hundred seventeen years?"

"Certainement. It is true."

I didn't want to ask about where he'd been before that. "You don't look that old."

I didn't want to hear his next words either.

"I assure you I am even older than that."

"And just how do you explain all of this?"

"Alors, it is quite simple. I am a vampire."

CHAPTER 5

New Orleans: 6:59 P.M. CDT

The clock on the marble table beside the bed chimes eight times. The sleeper throws back the covers and steps onto a black rug, thick as fur. His pajamas are black silk with a narrow satin stripe. His hair is the shade of midnight. He strides to the window and sweeps aside the heavy black velvet draperies. His eyes are dark craters in a face as white as the moon. He stares out into the shadowy street, listening, then nods to himself as he turns back to the room. The look on his face would make evil run whimpering like a dog from the room.

"Eugene. You have somehow managed to escape.

But you are no match for Louis Vennard. I will find you and this time I will finish you forever."

Wicklow, West Virginia: 8:01 P.M. EDT

Vampire! Vampire? At first I thought I wasn't hearing right. "Um, excuse me, but did I hear you say you are a . . . um . . . vampire?"

"Mais oui. I am a vampire."

I was losing it. "Um, how long have you been a vampire?"

"Since I was a young man."

He didn't look like he was joking. He believed he was a vampire.

"Prove it," I said.

He frowned. "Prove it?"

"Yes. Prove to me that you're a vampire." I was going to be scientific about this.

"What would you wish me to do?"

"Well, um, what should I call you? Mr. Car-on-de-lay?"

"Alors, if I have been in your house a week, we are old friends, non?"

I wanted to say no, that I didn't usually make friends that way but he went on. "My friends call me Eugene."

"My friends call me Jeff."

"And we are the friends, yes, Jeff?"

I didn't think so but I wasn't sure what he meant. "Okay, Eugene. Do your vampire stuff. We can start with your teeth. Show me your teeth."

He bared them in a sort of grin. They were long and yellowish and could use a good brushing and flossing but otherwise looked like, well, like teeth. "No vampire teeth here."

"I assure you they are vampire teeth."

I wasn't going to argue with him.

What else made vampires vampires? I thought of the mirror. Perfect. Vampires don't show up in mirrors. "Stand in front of my mirror, please, Eugene."

"Of course," he said, but he looked puzzled.

He stood in front of my dresser and looked at himself in the mirror, smoothing the hair on the back of his head and his mustache and brushing a piece of lint off his sleeve. Then he started to move away.

"Oh no you don't! You can't fool me." I jumped behind him. And there we were. One slightly chubby vampire with me right behind him both in the mirror.

"Your batting average isn't good, Eugene," I

told him. "How do you usually convince people you are a vampire?"

"I have never had to do so," he said.

"Well, now you do. Show me what makes you a vampire."

He shrugged and sort of hunched his neck into his collar and smiled. "Some vampires are more successful than others."

What made vampires vampires besides teeth and not being killable and all that stuff? They were supposed to be like bats. They were supposed to be aerodynamic. Inspiration. "Let's see you fly."

"Fly?"

"Fly. Vampires fly, don't they?"

"Mais oui. But I have how do you say it, the cramp from being in the trunk."

He was stalling. "Try, Eugene."

"I cannot just leap up from the floor and fly. I must have the perch to leap from."

I thought he might be right about that from vampires I'd seen in the movies. They unwrapped their capes and took off from high ledges. "Okay, climb up on the headboard of my bed."

He gave a little shrug and awkwardly climbed up on my bed and onto the headboard. It was the bookshelf kind. He stumbled over my clock radio, knocked a book onto the floor, and teetered on the shelf, but somehow managed not to fall. He pressed himself against the wall, palms flat against it. "I really don't do much flying," he said in a faint voice. "I don't care for the high places."

"It's your last chance to prove you are really what you say you are, a . . . um . . . vampire."

"Alors, if you insist." He closed his eyes and gave a little jump and at the same time pushed away from the wall with his hands.

It was pitiful. His chubby body went straight out, and he sort of bent in the middle. His feet sagged and then he fell straight down, face in the bedspread. He didn't even bounce.

I have to admit I was disappointed. It would be cool to have a vampire around. Somebody to talk to. To fly with.

Eugene got up with great dignity and straightened his clothes. "You must understand, I am out of the practice."

Did vampires have to train like athletes? Before I could ask, his stomach rumbled loudly. There was the answer. He was a homeless person just trying to make the best of a bad situation. He had somehow been living in my closet and got locked in there. Maybe he had even been in some sort of coma. He needed a good meal. Then I would send him on his way.

"Come on downstairs, Eugene," I said. "We have some leftover meat loaf I think you'd like to meet." I laughed but he didn't.

"Who is this Meetloof?"

"Meat loaf. Well, it's something to eat."

"Ah. That is good. I have much hunger."

As we went downstairs I tried not to think about all the little holes in my theory. Eugene was very well-dressed for a homeless person. His clothes were odd looking, but he had a gold watch chain hanging from his pocket. And then there was the weight problem. Eugene was chubby. How could he have been in the trunk a week and still be chubby? But maybe he had been twice as chubby last week and had lost weight in the trunk.

And the dust. What about the dust pile on the lid? Well, maybe we had made more dust with all our unpacking and cleaning. Then there's the bathroom problem. I didn't even want to think about *that.*

The key and the lock on the trunk flashed in my mind. And the skulls. An icicle slid down my spine.

CHAPTER 6

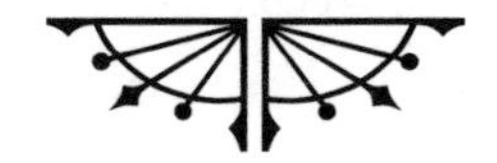

New Orleans: 7:57 P.M. CDT

Vennard wraps the cape around his tuxedo and steps into the narrow street of the French Quarter. The air is like warm soup and smells like coffee. On the sidewalk a woman in a shiny purple dress says, "Look, Harley, that guy's going to a Mardi Gras party."

"It ain't Mardi Gras yet, Pearl," Harley says.

Vennard is always hungry when he awakens. He needs a snack. He considers Pearl. Her face is smeared with bright makeup. Unappetizing. Vennard bares his fangs. Harley and Pearl hastily cross the street and disappear around the corner.

Wicklow, West Virginia: 8:58 P.M. EDT

The kitchen was fairly modern for an old house. The walls, floor, and appliances were white, sort of like the inside of a refrigerator, but Mom had hung fruit paintings around to brighten the place up and put a big blue bowl on the counter. It was filled with bananas, onions, and big knuckly bulbs of pungent elephant garlic. Garlic was a vampire repellent! If Eugene was really a vampire as he claimed, he would be unable to touch the garlic or maybe even to stay in the same room with it. Eugene hesitated in the doorway. Maybe the garlic was keeping him out. This would be a real test. I picked up the biggest bulb and tossed it to him. "Catch!"

He caught the garlic, then fumbled with it.

It worked! He couldn't hold it. He batted the garlic around in the air like it was a hot potato. But at last his fingers grasped the bulb. He didn't drop it. He didn't throw it away in horror. He looked at it. Then he sniffed. "Ah, garlic. Such an unmistakable odor. Excellent for curing the ague, fevers, calming the liver. And to flavor the stew."

Another flunked test. Eugene was just a klutz.

I heaped a plate with leftovers for him and

stuck it in the microwave. He stood holding the garlic bulb, looking around with wonder. “Is this a laboratory?”

Aha, the bathroom problem. “No, there’s a lavatory in the bathroom through the office down the hall.”

“Bath? Non, non, I mean is this a laboratory of science?”

“No, this is the kitchen. I am heating your food.”

“Where is the fire?”

“We don’t need one.” I explained about the microwave. “It’s like an oven but there’s no heat.”

He didn’t look convinced. “No heat. An oven without the heat. And the food, it will be warm?”

“Very warm.” I got him to sit down at the table but he still looked confused, like he’d never seen a kitchen before. Maybe he had amnesia and had forgotten what a kitchen was. Or maybe he wasn’t allowed in the kitchen at the mental hospital he had escaped from. I filled a glass of water from the tap and popped in a handful of ice cubes. He stared at it with fascination.

“How do you chip the ice in perfect little blocks?”

“We don’t chip it. It freezes that way.” I

opened the freezer door but he didn't seem to understand, just sat blinking and staring at the cubes.

I put a blue-checked placemat and a knife and fork on the table in front of him.

He was still looking at the glass of water. "Do you keep a slave at the pump day and night?"

"Slave?"

"To pump the water whenever you want it."

"No, I just turn on the tap." I showed him. "We don't have slaves."

"No slaves? What is this place?"

"Wicklow, West Virginia."

"The western part of Virginia? But Virginia is a slave state."

"No, I mean the state of West Virginia. Once it was part of Virginia, but it didn't secede from the Union with the rest of Virginia in the Civil War."

"The Civil War? Does that mean people were nice to each other?"

I grinned at his joke but he seemed serious. Didn't people wherever he came from know about the Civil War in the United States? "No, people killed each other. It was a horrible war. But it ended slavery forever in the United States."

"So if you have no slaves, how do you get the water?"

I launched into an explanation of municipal waterworks. I think he only understood the part about hand pumps but he nodded and said "Ah," as though he got it.

I folded a blue-flowered paper napkin beside the fork.

"What is this?"

"It's a napkin." Definitely from another planet.

He touched the edge. "It is paper. How do you wash it?"

"We don't. We throw it away after we use it."

"Throw it away." He marveled over that for a while. "You must use a lot of the paper."

"I guess." I didn't want to explain recycling.

The microwave pinged and I set the plate in front of him. He stuck his finger into the mashed potatoes and jerked it back when he discovered they were hot. I thought the meat loaf should have been raw, with him claiming to be a vampire. But it was the right color with all the tomato sauce on top. Maybe he thought it was raw because he ate all of it. He was still hungry so I microwaved two packages of popcorn and he ate that. Then I found a small steak in the freezer and defrosted it in the microwave. I slapped the plate in front of him.

"Pardon, Jeffrey, mais what is this?"

"Raw steak. It may be cooked just a little. That happens sometimes when you thaw it in the microwave. But it looks like it's got plenty of juice left in it."

He gave me a reproachful look. "I do not eat the bifteck raw. I like it well cooked, if you please."

"Okay." Some vampire he was, eating well-done meat. He'd flunked another vampire test. It would have been fun, a visit from a vampire. That sounded like the title of a book. I could write one about Eugene. It would be a great book, on the best-seller list for years. I put a little margarine in a frying pan and made blackened steak for this unbloodthirsty so-called vampire. It was a little more blackened than I intended, but Eugene said he preferred it that way.

"I thought vampires bit people and drank their blood."

"Some do. But not all. You have the good vampires and the bad vampires, just like anybody." He spread his hands. They didn't look like vampire hands, but I had only seen those in movies.

"You don't fly very well and you don't like high

places. You don't like raw meat. Garlic doesn't bother you. You show up in mirrors. You don't even have retractable teeth. What kind of vampire are you?"

"A good vampire, of course."

And a hungry one. That time in the trunk had given him a whopper of an appetite. I fried up some eggs to go with the steak and toasted half a loaf of bread. He ate a whole jar of crab apple jelly with it and drank two glasses of milk.

Wicklow, West Virginia: 10:59 P.M. EDT

A car turned into the driveway. Mom! She was going to be mad at me for not going to the Generos'. She would be extra mad if she found Eugene in the house.

"Quick! Go back up to my room and don't come down. Be real quiet."

"Mais, what—" He got up slowly.

"Hurry, and don't make any noise. Just go." I shoved him through the door and started throwing things in the dishwasher.

Mom came in with a stack of books. She dropped them on the table. "Hi, Jeff. Thanks for coming back to clean up for me. I've got to get better organized. Seems like I'm always in a rush and always behind. Did you have fun?"

She thought I'd been next door. I didn't correct her. It didn't seem like the thing to do. Maybe she wouldn't find out I hadn't gone.

"Yeah." Well, I did have fun. Sort of. "How was class?"

She yawned. "There's your answer. I stopped off at the library to get more books for my paper, but I'm too tired to work tonight. I think I'll go straight to bed."

Great. It would give me time to deal with Eugene. I finished the dishes and went up the steps two at a time. I didn't know what I'd find in my room. I didn't know much about the habits of vampires—or people who thought they were vampires. Maybe he was back in the trunk. Or gone. Maybe he had flown away out my window now that he'd had some food.

He was sitting in my chair reading a book. The hair on the back of my neck stood up as I remembered the skeleton of Ightham Mote. I looked at the book. *Robinson Crusoe.*

Eugene noticed me and closed the book without marking his place. "I know the ending," he said. "I read it when Danny first published it. I knew him when his name was Danny Foe. Interesting chap. Very imaginative."

I flipped the book open to find the publication date. London—1719. Daniel Defoe wasn't the only one with a lot of imagination.

It was time for the eleven o'clock news. I turned on the TV with the remote. Eugene yelped when Renata Diaz came on the screen with the news. He cowered behind the door, muttering in French between chattering teeth. It would have been funny if I hadn't been worried about Mom hearing him.

"Be quiet, Eugene. It's only the TV." I explained about airwaves. He just looked at me and stayed behind the door.

I watched for news about an escaped inmate or a vampire impersonator. But there were only the usual things, robberies, fires, the president welcoming the prime minister of Australia.

Eugene went up to the TV. He touched it with his finger, then jumped back as though he expected it to be hot like the mashed potato.

"This—this is the president?"

"That's him."

"But he doesn't look like Millard Fillmore."

"That's because he isn't Millard Fillmore."

Now Eugene looked at me. "Yesterday the twentieth of June, Millard Fillmore was the president. It was in the papers. When was the election?"

I studied him. He seemed genuinely distressed. He wasn't making this up. If he had been in an institution for a while and had just got out, wouldn't he think the president was somebody recent or famous, like Clinton or Kennedy or Lincoln? Why Millard Fillmore? Nobody would make up Millard Fillmore. Nobody's ever even *heard* of Millard Fillmore.

"There hasn't been an election for a year or two. Millard Fillmore was president—gosh I don't even know when, but I know it was in the last century."

"It was 1852. Yesterday was the twentieth of June 1852 and Millard Fillmore was president."

I looked at my watch. Today was the twenty-first of June and Millard Fillmore had been dead for at least 100 years.

This time a whole squadron of icicles went down my back.

CHAPTER 7

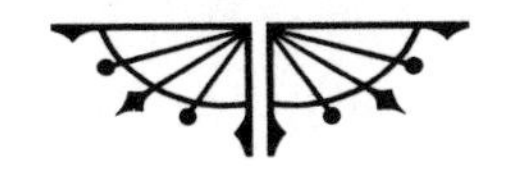

New Orleans: 10:59 P.M. CDT

Vennard enters the restaurant Sangfleur through velvet curtains the color of blood. He questions Felix about Carlotta. Felix has not seen her.

"And Eugene?"

"Your cousin, Eugene Carondelet?" Felix pauses. "No, Monsieur, I have not seen him since 1852." He seats Vennard at a small round table in the corner of the dining room. A waiter brings Vennard a goblet filled with ruby liquid. He sips it slowly. His eyes do not leave the curtains.

The waiter returns with his entrée. Vennard picks up his fork. He takes a bite of his steak tartare.

The meat is fresh and well ground, and the shade of red that only comes when raw.

Wicklow, West Virginia: 2:16 A.M. EDT

I gaped at Eugene for a while. I could accept his thinking he was a vampire. Sort of. I've heard of people who think they are Napoléon or Superman or other famous people. But Eugene didn't think he was famous. He thought he was a vampire. He thought he'd been in that trunk since 1852.

Finally I said, "Let me get this straight. You think you've been in that trunk since 1852."

"I remember the date precisement. It was the twentieth of June 1852. A warm night in New Orleans. My cousin Carlotta sent me a note to meet her at a warehouse on Magazine Street. But I could not find her. The dawn was coming and I was forced to seek accommodations."

"Yeah, right." I studied him. His brown eyes looked as innocent as a puppy's. He really believed all of this. "Okay, Rip Van Vampire. You went to a warehouse one night, climbed in a trunk, and woke up here almost 150 years later. Does this kind of thing happen to you a lot?" I thought he was acting pretty cool about it. I thought *I* was acting pretty cool about it.

"Not often, non. Once I slept for a week in a packing box. Alors, it was a prank when I was a child."

Some prank. "What did you dream about all those years?"

He looked me straight in the eye. "Vampires do not dream, my friend. Not when we are asleep. Unless there is something troubling. Moi, I never have dreams at night. Only dreams of the day."

I let that go by. I didn't think I wanted to know what vampires dream about when they are awake. Not even the dreams of a nice, ineffectual vampire like Eugene.

"Doesn't it bother you to have missed all those years?" Wait a minute. What was I saying? None of this was true. There were no vampires. Eugene himself was merely a figment of my imagination. I reached out and touched his sleeve.

Correction. A figment of my reality. There was no doubt he was real. I could feel the weave of the fabric of his coat, the solidity of his arm inside the sleeve. But was he a vampire or a nut? That was the question.

Or was he a nutty vampire?

"You do not believe me, non? Alors . . ." He reached into his pocket. "Ici, here is the note. See the date?"

I looked at the yellowed paper with its spidery brown writing. "It's in French."

"Pardon. The date is 20 juin 1852. That means the twentieth of June 1852."

"I can read the numbers." He could have written it himself, torn the page from the end of an old book, used diluted brown ink, copied nineteenth-century handwriting. But that seemed to be a lot of trouble to go to. I decided to treat him as a nonviolent vampire for the time being, until I could figure out what was going on. With the help of the TV, I gave Eugene a crash course on the highlights of the twentieth century which he had missed. It took most of the night. A lot had happened since 1852. Eugene was amazed, but he took to TV right away.

"And you say these people I am seeing with my own eyes are normal-sized people and not in the little TV box?" He peered closely at a rerun of the *I Love Lucy* show.

"That's right."

"They come through the air?"

"Well, yes, sort of."

"They are the witches, then?"

"No, no." I tried to explain. But it's a little fuzzy to me, too. It was getting late.

"I think I'll hit the sack," I told him.

"But what did it do to you?"

"No, it means I think I'll go to bed. You can stay up and watch TV if you want to."

"Merci. This Lucy, she is a funny lady, non?"

"The funniest." I yawned and showed him how to turn the TV off when he was ready to go to sleep. He was more interested in turning the TV on and off. *Click click.* Finally I had to tell him I couldn't sleep with him doing that.

"Where may I sleep?"

Not in my bed, I started to say, but then I remembered that vampires have to sleep in total darkness to avoid the light of day, which is bad for their complexions or something. I looked at the closet. The door was open. There was the trunk, its lid thrown back. Eugene followed my eyes.

"I do not think I want to go in that trunk again," he said. "I do not want to miss another century."

I thought about it. I couldn't put him in the guest room. If Mom found him there she would have a fit. Besides it wasn't dark enough.

"I guess you'll have to sleep in the bathtub," I said. I needed to show him where it was anyway for other reasons. I showed him the toilet. He was fascinated and flushed it three times before I explained that we had to pay for the water.

"Pay? Pay for water? I have never heard of such."

"We have to pay for almost everything now."

"Do you pay for the air?"

"No, it's free," I said.

The tub was extra large, old with claw feet and a curling lip. I put quilts and pillows in the tub. Then I made him place a quilt over the top of the tub so that he was covered and pulled the shower curtain around so nobody would notice anything unusual.

"It will be completely dark," I told him.

He plumped up the pillows and climbed in. His legs were a teensy bit too long but I propped them up with pillows.

"Comfy?" I asked.

He smiled sweetly. "Oui. It is so much more the luxury than folding oneself into a trunk."

I spread the quilt over the top and said good night to the vampire in my bathtub. It had been an interesting night.

Correction.
A weird night.
A crazy night.
A bizarre night.
A—you get the picture.

CHAPTER 8

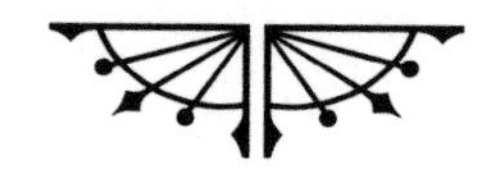

New Orleans: 1:03 A.M. CDT

Fog drifts like slow-moving ghosts through the French Quarter night. A woman's high-heeled footsteps echo through the deserted street. Vennard follows. "Carlotta," he whispers.

The footsteps turn into an alley off Dumaine Street. Vennard smiles. The alley is a dead end. He plucks a red rose from an ancient wall and sniffs it before tucking it into his lapel. Then he steps into the fog-shrouded alley.

Vennard emerges. She was not Carlotta, but now he has the energy to continue his quest. He carefully wipes his mouth on a red silk handkerchief and then walks swiftly away.

Wicklow, West Virginia: 9:12 A.M. EDT

Mom woke me up too early the next morning. "Jeffrey, we need to talk," she called from the bottom of the stairs.

I knew that tone. She had talked to Mrs. Gennero. I leaped out of bed and ran into the bathroom, slamming the door. I reached through the shower curtain and turned on the spray.

"I can't hear you," I said in what I hoped was the voice of someone in a shower.

Something sounded funny and it wasn't my voice.

The shower jets fell with thunderous thuds.

And then I remembered.

The quilt!

The vampire!

There was a vampire in my bathtub!

And my mother was knocking on the door.

"Jeffrey, what is that noise? What are you doing in there? Jeffrey, I'm coming in."

The handle turned.

I jumped through the curtain and pulled it shut behind me. I landed on top of Eugene who responded with a loud *whumphfff.* I'd probably killed him. But it was better than trying to explain him to my mother. At least he wouldn't make any noise.

But you can't kill a vampire. That's what all the vampire movies say. Except with a wooden stake through the heart or a silver bullet or something like that. I couldn't remember. I had more important things to deal with.

Like my mother.

She opened the door.

She was in the bathroom.

I pressed the shower curtain around my face and peered out at her. She couldn't see that I was still wearing my pajamas. She couldn't see that I was standing on a vampire wrapped in her great-grandmother's flowered quilt.

"Jeffrey, what are you doing?"

"Hi, Mom. I'm taking a shower. What does it look like I'm doing?"

"With you, I'm never sure. The water sounds funny. Jeffrey, you're not peeing in the shower, are you?"

"Mom!"

I slapped the curtain closed.

"Sorry. Come on downstairs when you are finished."

She left. I let the water run a few minutes. The quilt was already soggy. A little more wouldn't matter. Eugene was probably drowned if he wasn't squashed.

When she'd had time to get down the stairs, I turned off the faucet and climbed out of the tub. My pj's were soaked. I put on my jean shorts and a blue T-shirt and tiptoed to the linen closet in the hall. I pulled out a crazy quilt, which was more appropriate for Eugene anyway. In the bathroom I peeled back the wet flowered quilt. Eugene was peacefully snoring, a little motorboat putt putt. He opened one eye and squinted at me like he didn't know me.

I put a finger to my lips and said, "Shhh." He closed his eye and snored gently. He didn't seem to notice that light was falling on him. I don't think he was really awake. His clothes appeared dry. I spread the crazy quilt over him and rolled the wet one into a ball, stuffed it into a plastic bag, and stuck my pj's in with it. I pushed the bag into the cabinet under the lavatory. I'd have to dry the wet things on the line as soon as Mom left the house.

Downstairs Mom made me sit down for one of those Mom talks. You know the kind. Where she talks and you kind of mumble back because you don't want to say the wrong thing, but you're not sure what might set her off at that point so it's best to sort of make noises like you're agreeing with her.

She'd found out from Mrs. Gennero that I didn't go over there last night. She was disappointed in me. She couldn't count on me. Well, I couldn't count on her either. She was the one who had jerked me away from my life on Planet Earth and brought me here to the wilds of West Virginia. And it was wilder than anybody thought. If she knew we had a vampire upstairs in my bathtub. . . . I wondered for a split second if she would move back to Washington. But she had a teaching contract, had been married to a lawyer. Contracts were sacred. She would have Eugene carted off somewhere to a psycho ward. I tuned back in.

"Jeff, you're going to have to try harder to fit in here. I know it's different from your life in the city."

"Mmmmmbe-ummmmm."

"You have to understand. We can't go back. We have to make a new life."

I mumbled again.

"Jeff, do you have something in your mouth? Gum? Marbles? Crazy clay?"

"Noummmm." This usually worked, but not today.

"Well, speak up. We need to have a serious conversation and I can't have it with someone who sounds like a somnolent two-toed sloth with a mouthful of glue."

Mom's attempt at humor. I made a little smiley mouth.

"This is not a joke. Mrs. Gennero's offer is generous and the solution to my problem. I know Wicklow is a safe place, but I don't want to leave you alone at night."

I tried to explain why I didn't go to the Genneros', that I couldn't stand Alison, she was always spying on me, telling me what to do, that the only reason they asked me was so Alison would have somebody new to boss around. Mom didn't believe that but finally came around to see my point. But she was still hung up about leaving me in the house. If only she knew the truth.

"But Jeff, it just isn't safe for you to stay here alone. What if somebody broke in?"

I would just call my vampire and he would

take care of the intruder. I didn't think that would go over very big with Mom. Besides, Eugene wasn't much of a deterrent except maybe to a mouse. And I wasn't sure about that.

Instead, I gave her a list: (1) dial 911, (2) yell for help, (3) jump out of the upstairs window, (4) run to the Genneros'. "The same things I'd do if you were here," I finished.

"I just don't think you're trying to fit in here. Your refusal to go to the Genneros' is a symptom of your attitude. We're here, Jeff. This is where our life is. We have to stay here for a year. I signed a contract."

"*I* didn't sign a contract."

Mom studied me. We were in the kitchen. Time passed. A lot of time. I wanted to look at my watch. Instead, I just sat there, squirming inside, meeting her eyes on the outside. Then she said, "I'll talk to Angela," and went to her office. I heard her punching numbers on the phone.

Mom fixed it up with Mrs. Gennero that when she went to class, they would keep an eye on our house so I could stay home.

I walked to town to replace the food Eugene had eaten and got two frozen chicken dinners for him, microwave popcorn, and more bread. The groceries took a huge chunk out of my money stash. Although I hadn't had much to spend it on lately, I could see a problem developing with Eugene's eating habits. Maybe he would slow down when he had made up for all the years of not eating. I wondered how long that would take.

Bat Ears popped up from behind a rack of videos. Had she followed me without my noticing her?

"Hi, Jefferson!" she chirped. I picked up the bags and walked out of the store without speaking.

But she wouldn't let me ignore her. She caught up, her braces catching sunlight. "What did you do last night?"

Did she suspect something? "Um. I watched TV."

"You could have watched it at our house. We have a satellite dish and get about four hundred channels. My mom made a chocolate cake and a churn of ice cream before she knew you weren't coming over."

Satellite TV! Chocolate cake! Homemade ice cream! I thought about my favorite programs and felt a pang of emptiness right where the cake and ice cream would have gone. We only got two and a half channels. I almost said I would come over tonight, but that cake was too expensive. It would cost me my independence from Bat Ears. And, if I went over in the daytime, my mom would make me go over there at night. "I like old movies. We get plenty of those. And I had the lemon bread your mom made." The truth is I never even got a crumb. Eugene finished that, too.

We turned uphill on Stephens. She babbled on, telling me more about Wicklow than I ever wanted to know. Like we're the only teenagers in town. Why didn't that surprise me?

"We'll be riding the bus to school together in September."

"Oh, that's going to be loads of fun."

She ignored my sarcasm. Or maybe she didn't get it. "You'll like Wicklow Junior High. It's really cool."

I bet.

She stopped in front of her house but I kept going. I had things to do. Those froggy eyes stayed on my back.

As I put away the food, Mom said, "Was that Alison you were with?"

"Yeah. She followed me home."

"Oh. I see." Mom sounded like she was smiling. She probably thinks I secretly like Alison. I've got news for her. I can't stand Alison.

Correction.

I loathe Alison.

I stomped up to my room to map out my plan to get Eugene into flying shape and on his way. Except for the vampire thing, Eugene seemed normal. Inept, but normal.

When the sun went down, I woke Eugene up.

New Orleans: 8:01 P.M. CDT

Vennard leans over the balcony railing of the Pontalba Apartments to watch Jackson Square below. On the right the Mississippi River rushes past carrying boats filled with parties of people. The clock on St. Louis Cathedral glows like a ghostly face. He leaps nimbly to the railing, spreads his cape, and soars over the Square. A woman points. "Look at that big bird." Vennard turns with a flourish and circles high over the old French Quarter of the city. He returns to the Pontalba's third floor balcony where, thinking they are safe at such heights, unwary people often leave a door ajar.

Wicklow, West Virginia: 9:01 P.M. EDT

All those movies where vampires bound out of bed at dusk, gnashing their teeth, eager for fresh blood are a bunch of bananas. That is if Eugene really is a vampire. Because he was the worst sleepyhead I have ever met. As the sun began to go down I pulled back the quilt over the tub. Eugene snarled and tried to snatch it back.

"Come on, Eugene. It's time to get up."

"Egumpppfffxxx."

"Is that French?"

"L'egumpppfffxxx."

"Eugene, I don't speak French."

He rolled up into a ball and turned over. That was how he had fit into that trunk and why he was stiff after sleeping that way since 1852. Five minutes in that trunk could do it. But it was time to get up and exercise so he could fly again. If he ever had.

"Come on, Eugene, get up. It's almost dark outside and you need to eat so you can get strong."

"Grizzzzleegrummmmphxzzzz."

That wasn't French.

Finally I sopped a washcloth with cold water

from the lavatory and put it on his face. When he had sorted out his English, he said, "Never have I been so rudely awakened!"

Yesterday's awakening had been pretty rude with the baseball bat. I gave Eugene a pair of my dad's old running shorts and a T-shirt and told him to put them on. "Keep your shoes and socks on." I didn't have sneakers for him. He would have to work out in his own footgear.

In a few minutes the door opened and Eugene emerged yawning and stretching. He looked ridiculous but I managed not to laugh. The T-shirt was red with "Mt. Vernon 10K" on the front. Dad ran a lot before he met Moira. Said he was running off his frustrations. I wondered what he did now.

Eugene's legs sort of dangled from Dad's old navy shorts. His shoulders sagged, and his skin was frog-belly white. He pulled at the shirt where it stretched tightly over his rotund stomach.

"What is this, the bathing costume?"

"Exercise clothes. Now, Eugene, we're going to begin a serious exercise program so that you can get your strength back. First, I have to see what kind of shape you're in. Let me see you lift these weights."

"Lift those things? But why?"

"To tone up your muscles."

He reached down and tugged at the barbell. "It is very heavy. Why would anyone want to pick up such a thing?"

I lightened the weights but it was no use. Eugene couldn't budge the barbell. Or wouldn't. In the end I got a large can of fruit cocktail and one of pork and beans from the pantry and had him do arm curls with them. The cans weren't of equal weight, but they would have to do for now.

Eugene dropped the cans. They rolled under the dresser, the bed. He got stuck under the bed trying to get them out and I had to lift one end. I retrieved the cans after that. Finally I figured out he was dropping them on purpose. I heard another thump as I rolled out from under the bed, but Eugene was standing still in the middle of the room. "Did you make a noise?"

"Moi?" he panted.

It could be Bat Ears. I looked out the window. The Genneros' house was all lit up. Insects were clacking and doing their insect thing. Nothing seemed to be moving in the shadows under the trees. It must have been my imagination.

I started him on some calisthenics. But Eugene

couldn't even touch his toes. His stomach got in the way. His arms weren't long enough. His back hurt. He complained. Loudly. And his stomach growled.

"This is worse than the trunk. This is the torture, Jeff. Can I stop please?"

His griping got to me. I gave in and cooked him the chicken dinner hidden in the freezer behind a quart of strawberry sherbert. Eugene ate that, too. As his spoon scraped the bowl, I heard another noise.

"Did you hear that?"

"Moi? Non."

I was getting jumpy. Somebody must be out there. Bat Ears. But I couldn't see anything. I thought I heard a twig snapping, the crush of leaves under a foot. It could have been a cat. Or a raccoon. Or a werewolf. Or almost anything. I mean, look what I had found inside the house.

CHAPTER 9

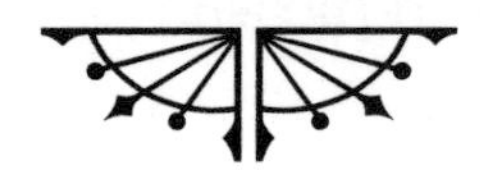

New Orleans: 3:37 A.M. CDT

The *Times-Picayune* headline in a corner kiosk: "Tourist Drained in French Quarter Alley."

At the Sangfleur, Felix tries to calm Vennard. "Eugene has not been seen all these years. I'm sure he's gone forever. You do not have to worry about him turning up again."

"What do you know about anything?" Vennard snarls. His hand snakes out and grabs Felix's throat.

"Party. Grossard's," Felix croaks.

The talon of a hand relaxes.

Wicklow, West Virginia: 12:37 A.M. EDT

"... and this beautiful blue Altgelland diamond ring surrounded by six, count them, six pinpoint diamonds can be yours at the amazing price of $24.95. Their brilliance will dazzle your family and friends. You will be the star of the neighborhood. But don't stop there. You can be a princess in the matching tiara, pendant, and bracelet for little more than the cost of an evening's meal. Yes, that's right. For just pennies you can be royal."

I groaned and turned over, pulling the pillow over my head.

Mom said we couldn't afford a satellite dish and cable didn't come to Wicklow, so we were stuck late at night with the shopping shows, reruns of game shows, and old movies. Eugene had become a TV addict, a home-shopping junkie, a game-show fiend, and an old movie buff. He was in love with Lana Turner, Ava Gardner, Rita Hayworth, and Marilyn Monroe. If this kept up, I would have to take up vampire hours in self-defense, sleeping all day and staying up all night.

Except that I had to wash the clothes and that meant sheets and towels, too. Then I had to fold and put them all away to keep Mom from discovering Eugene sleeping in my bathtub. She was suspicious at first and then pleased with my attempts at housekeeping. I made a lemon icebox pie to show her what a good boy I was. It looked more like lemon icebox soup, but it tasted great and that's what counts.

But my nights were something else.

Wicklow, West Virginia: 1:05 A.M. EDT

The sound of someone crying woke me. I jumped up. Eugene was sitting in my chair, sobbing. The TV flickered in black and white, the sound turned low. "What's the matter, Eugene?"

Tears ran down his face. He pointed at the TV. Leslie Howard stood on the guillotine. "It is a far, far better thing I do than I have ever done before," he was saying. I recognized *A Tale of Two Cities* from my last English class.

"It's just an old movie, Eugene."

"Non, non, it is my friend, Sidney Carton. I did not know what happen to him. Now I know. He was beheaded in the French Revolution." He sobbed again. I got a roll of toilet paper out of the bathroom and he blew his nose. Loudly.

"But it isn't real, Eugene. It was a book before it was a movie, something made up."

"Mais oui. The book was about a true person. Sidney was real. My friend."

"Look, Eugene, writers take real people and make up things about them. Sidney probably lived to a ripe old age and had lots of children and grandchildren. And great-grandchildren," I added for emphasis.

He looked at me with his red eyes. "You think this?"

"I know this. Writers came to my school all the time and told us how they make up their stories. All of them said they take true things and change them around, add stuff to make the stories more dramatic and exciting. It wouldn't be very dramatic to have old Sidney go off and open a McDonald's—er—café on the Left Bank and marry the baker's daughter, now would it?"

"Mais non." He sniffed and dried his face on his sleeve.

Eugene couldn't tear himself away from the old movies. I gave up around three and went to bed. I couldn't sit up with a vampire at night and impersonate a teenager during the day.

Wicklow, West Virginia: 9:11 A.M. EDT

Footsteps ascended the stairs. Mom! I jumped up and galloped into the bathroom.

"Jeffrey," she called outside the door. "Are you all right?"

"Sure, Mom. Why wouldn't I be?"

"It's late. You're usually ravenous by this time and down in the kitchen trying to eat everything in sight."

"Oh um, I had a snack last night," I said through the door.

"I noticed that a lot of food has been disappearing. The strawberry sherbert. I thought you didn't like strawberry."

"I don't." I thought fast. "But it's not bad with chocolate syrup poured over it."

There was a snort. Somewhere in the vicinity of the bathtub. "Oh. Well, I guess it would be. Especially if you added a banana and nuts. Like a split."

I opened my mouth. Then I remembered. We didn't have any bananas. "Yeah. I'll try that the next time. When you get some bananas." Was Mom suspicious? Was this a Mom trick?

"That's right. I forgot we didn't have any."

She didn't sound suspicious. Mothers are forgetful creatures. Everybody knows that. But I would have to be careful.

"What is that awful smell?"

"What smell?"

"Like something dead."

I looked around. I sniffed. There was a bad smell in the bathroom. I checked the toilet. Nope. It had been flushed. Finally I said, "Um, Mom, I am in the bathroom." I hoped I had put it delicately enough for her.

"Are you coming down soon?"

Eugene let out another snort. It ended in a distinct snoring sound. It was loud.

Correction.

Very loud.

"What was that?"

"I didn't hear anything." I flushed the toilet to cover up any more Eugene noises.

Footsteps led away from the door. I let my breath out. I didn't even know I was holding it. I peeked at Eugene. Sleeping like a baby vampire.

I checked myself in the mirror. Bags under my eyes. I looked more like a vampire than Eugene did. I felt like a zombie. I had to do something about his TV habit. And I would have to make him take a shower. That smell was probably Eugene. He hadn't had a bath all those years in the trunk. And his clothes hadn't been washed either.

I splashed my face with cold water and went downstairs to face the day. There were not many choices in Wicklow without malls, Internet, and only two and a half TV channels. I settled on a blanket under a tree with a book I'd asked Mom to get from the college library, *Vampire Lore* by Ursula von Bismarque. It was the usual stuff except that I found out the original vampires had been people in Transylvania with a blood disorder that made them pale and needing to drink blood. From that they evolved into supernatural beings who lived forever.

"What are you reading?"

I didn't have to look up.

Bat Ears squinted those green frog eyes. "Vampires! You don't believe in that stuff."

"There is a scientific basis for them," I said.

"You probably read all that Merlin stuff, too."

As a matter of fact, I do, but I wasn't going to tell her. "My mom brought it home for me."

That shut her up.

"Want to come over? My mom made chocolate angel food."

Chocolate angel food cake! I couldn't imagine anything better. But I wouldn't give in. "No thanks."

"Are you allergic to chocolate?"

"No, I'm allergic to you."

"That's dopey. People aren't allergic to people."

I gave her a look. She was right. I was allergic to her personality. I didn't like *her.* Why didn't she get it? She gave me a look back and got up.

"See ya."

The day really stretched out after that. I plowed through the book, learning a lot about vampires but feeling awfully lonesome along the way.

CHAPTER 10

New Orleans: 8:00 P.M. CDT

The clock strikes the hour but Vennard has long been awake, pacing the floor. He dresses quickly and carelessly. One of his ruby shirt studs is only half through the buttonhole. His black hair is tangled on the back of his head. He throws the cape about his shoulders and hurries out into the dusky night. He will find Carlotta and then he will finish Eugene.

Wicklow, West Virginia: 9:32 P.M. EDT

I woke Eugene up and made him put on his training clothes.

"Not again," he muttered, burrowing under the quilts.

I jerked them all the way off.

"I am so how-do-you-say so-ar?" he whined.

I hardened my heart. "You are flabby, Eugene. A disgrace to vampires. You can't fly. You can't touch your toes. You can barely walk—make that waddle—from the kitchen to the TV." I felt like a marine drill instructor. But Eugene had to fly again or I would be shelling out for food forever.

"Why do I have to fly when now we have the airplanes?"

"Because you have to fly to prove you are a vampire."

"Mais, why? I know I am a vampire. If you do not believe that, I cannot help it. I prefer to take flying lessons and fly a plane like Jimmy Stewart in *The Spirit of St. Louis.*"

I looked at him. There was no resemblance to Jimmy Stewart. But it gave me an idea. "You have to be fit to be a pilot. Do you think you are fit?"

He looked down at himself and shook his head.

"Come on, then, get into your gear and let's go. We'll try something different tonight to speed up the process. And bring your clothes."

Eugene stumbled out of the bathroom in his exercise gear, carrying his clothes. He looked pitiful. Not a muscle showing in his arms and legs. I wondered if he had *ever* been able to fly. But I had to get him into some sort of shape fast. I needed my allowance. I needed my sleep. I couldn't keep a vampire around forever. My mother would be sure to find him eventually.

We deposited his clothes in the washing machine. I dumped in the soap and turned it on the usual cycle.

"Is this another channel?" he asked, looking in the window. I explained about washing machines and dryers.

"So now instead of the servants you have the machines."

Progress. He was learning.

I eased open the back door and went outside. All the frogs and crickets in West Virginia were out there screeching their lungs out. I checked the Genneros' house. Not much light. No sign of Bat Ears, but you never know. We waited a while but nothing moved.

"Okay," I told Eugene. "Let's go."

I made him run in place to warm up and stretch.

"For what do I stretch? I am tall enough."

"Nobody is ever tall enough," I told him. "You could grow to be the tallest vampire in the world."

"There is already the tallest vampire in the world," he said, groaning and stretching. "He is my cousin, Louis Vennard." He clapped his hand over his mouth and looked around fearfully.

"What's the matter?"

"Nothing, I hope. I should not have said that name. He is evil."

"One of the bad vampires you told me about?" I teased.

"It is not funny, Jeffrey. He is the most evil in all the world. He is the reason I am a vampire."

"Who is this Venn—"

Eugene's hand clapped over my mouth. "Don't say that name. He has powers. He can hear the thought whispering on the wind, he can spit and put out a star, he can . . ."

"Okay, okay, I get the picture. He's a bad dude."

"The worst," Eugene said morosely. "He made me a vampire and my chère Carlotta so he can play with us like a cat with a mouse. But Carlotta and I made plans to escape together."

"When and where was this?"

"New Orleans in 1852."

Somebody else had mentioned New Orleans to me lately. Or maybe I heard it on TV while Eugene watched.

"How could he make you a vampire? I thought vampires were born that way, like having blue eyes or blond hair."

"No, no. We were ordinary people. Well, not exactly ordinary. But we weren't born vampires. He bit us."

"How did Ven—oops, sorry. How did he become a vampire?"

"He got into a bad group at the University of Paris. The initiation turned him into a vampire in the fourteenth century."

Sort of like joining a gang today.

"But if you are cousins, doesn't it run in the family?"

"Mais non. I am much younger than my cousin. Born in a different century, the fifteenth. Carlotta, aussi. I am sure he was responsible for my long sleep." He smiled wanly. "Just like in the movie. *The Long Sleep.*"

"It was *The Big Sleep.*"

"Yes, it was a big sleep."

And just like that, I believed him. It wasn't any big moment. He didn't prove it by flying or even by giving me a lot of details about vampire life or New Orleans in 1852. It was the joke that did it. I didn't think a delusional person would make a joke about *The Big Sleep*. Maybe I had been believing him even before the joke and hadn't admitted it to myself. That's a pretty weird thing to admit. There was Eugene in my dad's old running gear, learning about the modern life and probably doing a better job than I would be if the situation were reversed and I suddenly woke up in 1852. He was having to learn all the progress made since then while I would have to unlearn it all, forget about TV and computers and bathrooms or risk being chained up in a madhouse.

"Okay, you're limber enough. We're going to run."

"Run? Where will we run?"

"Nowhere. We're going to run just to be running."

"Mais, Jeff, that is comique. Why does one run if one is not in a hurry and not going anywhere?"

"So you can fly again. Running is good for you."

"How does the running make me fly?"

"Increases your stamina. Makes you stronger. You can't fly because you are weak from being in the trunk all those years. That is, if you ever really could fly."

"Oui, oui, I could fly. Not well, you understand, or far, but I could fly. Carlotta and I often took the little evening flight."

"So you say, but now you can't. So you have to exercise to get stronger. And that means running."

"Alors, okay." He shrugged and we took off at a trot down Stephens Street. Eugene had a curious little run, more like a hop that had its own rhythm, lippity leap, lippity leap. So he lippity leaped down Stephens and soon I found myself lippity leaping with him. At the foot of the hill, we turned right. I hoped if anybody saw us, they would just think we were out for an evening run. I'd never seen anybody running in Wicklow, but they had probably heard of it.

It was eerie being in beautiful downtown Wicklow at night. The place was empty.

Correction.

The place was empty in the daytime. Now it was deserted. So why did I feel that someone was watching us. Or something? The cemetery was behind us. Nobody was watching us from there. I hoped.

No, these eyes felt definitely alive. I glanced over my shoulder but saw nothing. Eugene had begun to pant now that we had left the steep downhill and reached level ground.

"Please, Jeff, I am very tired."

I ignored him.

"Jeff, I am dying."

I prodded him from behind. "Not yet, Eugene. Keep going just a little more."

But I decided to let him stop at the end of the next block. I mean, who knows about the heart of a multi-centenarian vampire? People should have medical checkups before they start a program of exercise, but I couldn't very well take him to a doctor. I could imagine how it would go.

"How old are you, Mr. Carondelet?"

"Four hundred and eighty-seven."

"I see."

And that would be the end of that. They would cart Eugene off to the funny farm and I could save my allowance for a kayak. But I couldn't do that to Eugene. I liked my way better. I would build up his strength so he could fly back to New Orleans or wherever he wanted to go.

"Okay, Eugene. We'll walk a while."

We stopped and he collapsed onto the sidewalk, right on the pavement. I checked. He was still breathing.

"Eugene?"

"Groan."

"How do you feel?"

"Groan."

"Okay, up. We'll walk now to cool you off." A good brisk walk was almost as good as running. The Frizzeria was still open so I made Eugene wait in the shadows and bought a fudge milk shake to perk him up. I bought myself one, too. We needed the protein.

On the way back we skirted the edge of the cemetery. I glanced at the shadowy tombs and headstones. It was almost as dead as downtown Wicklow. How do people know they have died in Wicklow? They can't go to the Frizzeria anymore.

As I was about to laugh at my own joke, something moved under a hemlock tree. Someone definitely was watching.

"Don't move," I hissed. Eugene froze.

"It is Vennard. He has found me," he moaned.

It was worse. Well almost as bad. It was Bat Ears.

"Run!" I yelled at Eugene.

We raced around the cemetery and up Stephens. I couldn't hear her behind us but she had to be there, braids bouncing, braces gleaming in the moonlight. Why couldn't I hear her?

Bat Ears waited on my porch. She wasn't even panting.

We ran around to the back door. I shoved Eugene in and slammed the door behind us.

"Hey!" Bat Ears yelled, pounding on the door.

I locked the door and pulled down the shades.

"Open up!"

"Not by the hairs of my chinny chin chin."

Wicklow, West Virginia: 10:04 P.M. EDT

I showed Eugene how to turn the shower on. He protested, saying he didn't like to be rained on, he liked to soak in the bubble bath, but there wasn't time before Mom would be home. It was lucky for Eugene that she was too busy with her classwork to notice there was a vampire sleeping in my bathtub.

I threw the wash into the dryer and left it to tumble. Then I put chicken and a pot of rice on to cook. For vegetables he could have a can of peas. I decided to limit his diet. He didn't look very aerodynamic and I thought perhaps weight was part of his trouble. I shouldn't have bought him that milk shake.

Eugene came down wearing his quilt. I explained my theory about weight to him as he cleaned his plate. The run had made him extra hungry.

"Mais non, Jeff. I am always the pudge. I could fly quite nicely before I fell asleep in the trunk. So, if it is not too much trouble, could I have the dessert, please? A little sherbert or cake?" he pleaded.

"You've already had a milk shake."

"That was not dessert. That was milk."

"It was calories, Eugene."

"Calories?"

I was saved by the dryer buzzer. I pulled his warm dry clothes out of the machine and presented them to him. "There you are, Eugene. Washed and dried in little more than an hour. Bet you couldn't do that in 1852."

"Mais non, Jeff."

I cleaned up the kitchen as he went into the downstairs bathroom to change back into his vampire suit.

"Jeff-rey! Your machines make my clothes small," he wailed.

He looked like Buster Brown. His suit had shrunk. The sleeves reached his elbows. His pants had turned into Bermuda shorts. And his rotund stomach smiled at me between his shirt and pants.

It was a disaster.

Actually, it was worse than that because I didn't have any more clothes for him. He certainly couldn't leave here looking like that. Vampire or not, Eugene had his dignity.

It was a dilemma. And I didn't have a solution. I sent Eugene back to my room. Mom came in as I finished up the kitchen.

"Hi, Jeff." She ruffled my hair as I dried a pot. She gave me one of those little Mom speeches designed to stroke the kid so he will feel good about himself. They usually work. This one almost did. "You've really been great. It's wonderful to have someone sharing the housework. I saw that mountain of laundry you put away last night. I'm so glad you've decided to make the best of things. And I'm glad that you are changing your mind about Alison. She's a nice friend and can introduce you to other kids."

"Wha-at?"

"Mrs. Gennero told me that Alison has been busy with you." She wandered off into her office to put away her books, leaving me with my mouth open to trap flies between my teeth.

I closed my mouth. Alison busy with me. What did she mean?

CHAPTER 11

New Orleans: 1:01 A.M. CDT

Vennard approaches the elegant columned house. He lifts the heavy brass gargoyle knocker and lets it fall with a single massive thud. A butler opens the door, but Vennard pushes past him to a roomful of men in black tuxedos and women in satin and jewels. The guests fall silent as Vennard enters. "Where is she?" he snarls.

"Carlotta does not wish to see you," the host tells him. "You know that. You have known that for four hundred years."

Another says, "We will not betray her."

Vennard's hand lashes out. He jerks the man by his shirtfront. The ruby studs pop out and hit the marble floor—*ping, ping, ping.* Vennard drops him in a heap.

"Do not thwart me," he hisses. The other vampires cower, helpless against his evil power.

Wicklow, West Virginia: 2:17 A.M. EDT

"Jeff, my friend, wake up. Quick! Quick!"

I struggled out of a comfortable dream of fishing with my dad to find Eugene bent over me, shaking my arm.

I bolted upright and looked around for Mom but she wasn't there. "What is it, Eugene?"

"We must do something. Atlanta is on fire."

"What?"

"Atlanta is burning. To the ground. No one seems to know. We must do something."

I struggled to understand his words. It didn't make sense. Atlanta on fire. "Eugene, how do you know this?"

"Look for yourself. It is on the TV. I see it in living color. It is real like the game shows and the news, not like the black-and-white movies you told me were not true."

I looked at the TV. Rhett Butler was lashing the horse while Scarlett hung on for dear life as they rode through the burning streets. Atlanta was really on fire. Only trouble was, it was a film clip from *Gone with the Wind.*

"Eugene, calm down and let me explain." But how to make him understand which programs were real and which were not? He was like a little kid. He thought he had it figured out, the ones in color were real and the black-and-white movies were fake. I was too tired to explain. "It takes practice, Eugene. You'll get it. Now let me get some sleep, okay?"

"Okay, Jeff. Sleep tight. Don't let the bugs bite."

Oh, brother.

Wicklow, West Virginia: 8:57 A.M. EDT

Someone knocked on the door downstairs. I woke instantly and jumped out of bed. The TV was off. I ran in the bathroom and peeked at Eugene, sleeping in his shrunken clothes.

Downstairs Mom was talking to the United Parcel deliveryman. "I didn't order a dust buster from Cyclone Appliances or anybody else."

"Do you refuse delivery then?" said an unknown voice.

"I certainly do."

She closed the door. I went down the stairs.

"The nerve of some companies. They just send a product out and think the recipient will accept it and pay for it." She went back into her office.

I didn't think about the dust buster. I had other problems. The smell in my bathroom for example. It had gotten worse. I sniffed around. It wasn't Eugene. He was clean, his clothes were clean. And then I remembered.

I opened the cabinet under the lavatory sink. The plastic bag fell out. It smelled like roadkill. The flowered quilt and my pajamas were all moldy. I would have to wash them tonight after Mom left. I stuffed them back under the lavatory.

I'd forgotten about the dust buster until the postman came with a delivery from Altgelland Jewels, Inc., and a foam cutter and suddenly the answer came to me.

Correction.

The answer hit me like a meteor out of the sky—or out of the Home Shopping Network.

I refused the packages, keeping my voice down so Mom wouldn't hear me. I marched upstairs to the bathroom, reached for the quilt and stopped. I didn't know what would happen if I woke up a sleeping vampire in the daytime. Would he yell or argue? Or turn to stone or catch fire? I decided to wait until dark.

Wicklow, West Virginia: 8:21 P.M. EDT

Mom's car hadn't cleared the driveway when I woke Eugene up. "Are you crazy? What do you mean ordering that stuff?"

"Pardon? Pardon?" Eugene looked up at me with his little brown vampire eyes opened as wide as they would go.

"I mean ordering that stuff from the Home Shopping Network. The dust buster and the jewelry and the foam cutter."

"But, Jeff, everybody needs a foam cutter." Eugene rubbed his eyes. "They say this is the thing to do. Just pick up the phone and call. I push all the buttons just as they say and a voice tells me what to do. They say they send it, see Odie. Odie means fast."

"No, no, Eugene. COD. It means 'cash on delivery.'" I gave him his exercise clothes, clean and dry and smelling fresh, not like a vampire had been sweating in them. I carried the plastic bag down to the laundry room and put the offending quilt and my pajamas in the wash.

Eugene complained with every breath that he didn't get enough sleep.

"I don't get enough either, not since you came here." I made him a pizza. I was tired of cooking special meals for a vampire. He could eat like the rest of us. Mom got these frozen pizza crusts and I piled on the toppings: tomato sauce, sliced tomato, cheese, black olives, garlic, onions, pepperoni, baked beans, whatever I could find. Eugene loved it. I made two more for him and another one for me.

Tonight we would exercise inside. I didn't want another run-in with Bat Ears. I'd bought an exercise video, Lydia LaVine's Lalarobics, I'd found on sale at the grocery. Lydia was a gorgeous blonde in a lavender leotard and lavender-tinted shiny tights. A purple-sequined sweatband held back her long silky hair. I shoved the video into the VCR.

"Today we will make our muscles move like liquid," she purred.

Eugene stared, in a trance. I couldn't get him to move.

"She . . . she . . . that . . . that . . ." he sputtered.

"Yes, exactly. But once she had muscles like you. She was a puny weakling and other girls kicked sand in her face at the beach. But now she is rich and beautiful and famous and so can you be if you do these exercises."

"Moi? I can have the muscles?"

"Of course you can, Eugene. The TV says so. You can believe it if the TV says it's so."

"Mais oui," he murmured.

He couldn't stop staring at Lydia.

"You like her, Eugene?"

"She is like a goddess, non?"

"Yes. Why don't you pretend you're dancing with her."

"Moi? I can dance with her? She would dance with a vampire?"

"Yes, even a 487-year-old one. Just do everything she does. You can dance, can't you?"

"But of course. I am French."

"Oh, right. I forgot."

Eugene was having the time of his life pretending he was dancing with Lydia.

"She has the good rhythm, don't you think?" he said as he bounced and jiggled along with Lydia.

"The best."

He didn't notice he was out of breath. He forgot to be tired. This was the answer to Eugene's training problem. Lydia and I would soon have this vampire in shape and ready to fly out of here. My vampire troubles were over.

Correction.

My vampire problems weren't even off the ground.

I looked up from watching Eugene to see a face staring through the second-floor window. There was no mistaking that hair, those pickle-green frog eyes. This time the frogs seemed to be jumping out of them straight at me.

CHAPTER 12

New Orleans: 9:33 P.M. CDT

Carlotta escaped from Vennard while her friends delayed him. Now they are on his hit list. For too long Vennard has been lax with the vampire community. He will remedy that. But first that puppy, Eugene, must be dealt with.

Wicklow, West Virginia: 8:04 P.M. EDT

I whipped the curtains closed. Too late. Bat Ears had seen everything. She banged on the window. "Open up!"

Eugene stopped dancing. He looked scared. "Jeff, is it the cops?"

She had seen Eugene. In my house. She would tell her mom and her mom would tell mine. That would mean big trouble. I would have to stay at the Genneros'. I wondered if it was against the law to harbor a vampire. "No, Eugene. Why do you think it's the cops?"

"That is what the cops say on the TV. 'Open up,' they say. 'I know you're in there.' Just like that."

"It's not the cops," I assured him. "It's worse. It's Bat Ears."

"You'd better let me in," she yelled. "If you don't, I'm telling. I'll write an article for the *Gistville Gazette.* Now open this window."

I pulled back the curtains and raised the screen. Alison stepped through it from the tree she'd climbed. I should have guessed she'd given up too easily. She'd been spying on us all along. Those were her eyes in the cemetery. And she'd heard everything tonight through those bat ears.

"This is Eugene," I told her.

Eugene gave a little bow. "Eugene Aloysius Pierre Phillippe Carondelet. And you are Mademoiselle Bat Ears."

She glared at me. "Mademoiselle Alison Annette Gennero, Monsieur Carondelet." She said some stuff in French.

She even had a French accent. They chatted away for a while. It was boring.

Correction.

It was like I wasn't even there.

"How do you know French?" I rudely interrupted her trilling verbs.

"I had it in school for years. It is my best subject—after literature, of course."

The question was, what was she going to do now: tell my mother, tell hers, write an article? Post it on the Internet? I put it into words. "What are you going to do?"

"Eugene has explained it all to me."

Eugene? They were on a first-name basis already. "Are you going to tell? About him being a vampire?"

She pricked up her bat ears. I swear they were beginning to look pointed. "Him being a what?"

Eugene was distressed. "The jig is up, Jeff. I tell her that I am your uncle visiting. I do not mention that."

Alison slitted her eyes and aimed them at me. "What's going on here? You'd better tell. I'll find out anyway."

"Do we have to come clean, Jeff?"

I nodded. "He's a vampire," I told her.

"Would you like to explain that further?"

"He's a vampire. What else can I say?"

She gave me a hard look. On the TV, Lydia LaVine did Lalarobics to her bouncy music. "A lot."

"Okay." I took a deep breath. I explained. About the closet, the keys, the trunk. I told her Eugene's age. His aerodynamical problem. His training program.

"His what?"

"Show her, Eugene."

"Pardon?"

"Give her a flying demonstration."

Eugene climbed up onto my headboard and repeated his pitiful demonstration of failure to fly.

Alison looked at us like we had lost our marbles. Maybe we had. There are cases of mass psychoses. Maybe Eugene and I constituted a mass.

"Well, this certainly explains a lot," she said, "I thought you were practicing to join a circus or something. But I'm not sure I believe you."

That was okay. I wasn't sure I believed it all myself.

She turned to Eugene. "Are you really a vampire?"

Eugene looked at her with his puppy-brown eyes and droopy mustache. "It is true," he said sadly. "But not a very good one."

I guess those eyes got to her. "Oh, you poor thing."

"Go back to your dancing," I told Eugene. I took her out in the hall and explained my problem. "He's really a nice guy, but he eats too much. I have to buy his food out of my allowance I was saving to buy a kayak."

She didn't look sympathetic.

Correction.

She looked unsympathetic. Like I picked up bunnies by the ears or something equally horrible.

"I don't get much sleep either," I added.

She ignored that. "I think you are selfish. How would you like it if somebody had locked you into a trunk for almost a hundred and fifty years and then all your rescuer could think about was a kayak?"

I started to say it sounded pretty sensible to me, but she interrupted. "I'll help you get food for him and train him. His physical condition is poor and he needs building up. Maybe his delusions, if that's what they are, are caused by malnutrition. When he's in better physical shape, the mental thing might go away. Or he'll be able to fly, proving that he really is a vampire. In either case, your problem will be solved."

Dr. Bat Ears to the rescue.

Wicklow, West Virginia: 10:33 A.M. EDT

Voices woke me up. Eugene had forgotten to turn off the TV. Eugene had forgotten to close the bathroom door. Footsteps on the stairs. Mom was coming!

I turned off the TV.

I closed the bathroom door and met Mom in the hall. I continued downstairs. She followed. "Jeff, why did you wash my great-grandmother's quilt?"

I poured myself a glass of milk, thinking fast. It was hard. But I managed. I'd had a lot of practice lately.

"It was smelling up the upstairs," I said. "I tracked the smell to the linen closet. The quilt was damp and moldy."

It sounded logical to me.

Luckily, it sounded logical to Mom, too.

A week went by. Things were a lot easier for

me with Bat Ears sharing the food problem. And everything. She even helped me head off deliveries of a set of drums, two sets of encyclopedias, enough Amberwax to wax the entire town of Wicklow, and a walking stick with a headlight.

Wicklow, West Virginia: 10:32 P.M. EDT

Bat Ears brought over a can of pineapple, two slices of anchovy pizza, a jar of pickles, and half a package of salted peanuts. Not exactly a balanced meal. But she had done her part. I had to give her that.

"It was the best I could do. Mom has noticed that food is disappearing. I don't know how much longer I can do this."

"Welcome to the club."

But she wasn't ready to give up on Eugene yet. She'd helped with his training program, starting out with high hopes that had dwindled.

"Just one little knee bend, Eugene. You can do it."

He groaned. In French. It sounded like English only with an accent.

I sat down to watch.

Eugene held on to the back of a chair with one hand. Bat Ears held his other hand as he bent his knees slowly. The room crackled with clicks, like castanets, as his knees popped.

"Good, Eugene," Bat Ears encouraged. "Now pull yourself upright."

But he couldn't do it and I had to help him.

"All right. Let's try a plié. It's French. It'll be easier for you."

Again he went down but not so far.

Again I had to help him up. He fell into the chair, panting. There was a lot of ham in that French vampire.

"Do something else, okay? I can't keep pulling him up. He weighs a ton."

"Jeffrey, we need to talk."

We went downstairs while Eugene did arm curls with a can of V-8 juice.

I'd been waiting for this. "Yes?" I said crisply, enunciating every letter as we reached the kitchen.

"This is not working out. I've used up my allowance for the week and sneaked stuff out of my house. This can't go on. If I dip into my savings, I'll be broke before Saturday."

"Yes?" I said again. "You would let a little

thing like that stop you from helping this poor benighted being?" Whatever benighted meant. It sounded good.

She shook her head. The red braids whipped around her back. "We need another plan. Something that works faster than just getting him into shape. We don't even know if he ever could fly. He says he could, but he might just be ashamed because all the other vampires fly."

She seemed to be buying the vampire thing. Eugene was very convincing. "So you believe him?"

"Well, not entirely. But there is that medical evidence of people needing blood in Transylvania."

"Eugene is French. He's never been to Transylvania. He doesn't even like rare meat."

She tossed her braids impatiently. "Whatever. His appetite is too big. He eats more than my whole family."

"He has a lot of catching up left."

She glared at me.

"Okay, so what do you want to do? Get rid of him? Take him out on the highway and leave him like people do with pets they are tired of?"

"No, of course not. We can't turn him out. We don't know what would happen to him. He might get hit by a car or put in jail. I've been thinking about it and I've decided we need help. If we accept that he's a vampire, then we have to admit there must be other vampires. And they probably all know each other. It's probably like belonging to some kind of club. They'd know what to do with Eugene. So I put an ad in the *Gazette.* When a vampire shows up, we'll turn Eugene over to him to go live wherever vampires live."

"You did WHAT!"

"I put an ad—"

"I heard that. What did you say, Wanted: Vampire. Send résumé?"

"Exactly!"

"Did you post it on the Internet?"

"No. I didn't think that was a good idea."

Neither was the first one. "Did you use my address?"

"Of course."

"So now all we have to do is wait to see what turns up at my door."

"Don't worry. I'll be here to help. And if anybody here notices the ad, they'll think it's a joke or something. We'll say it's for a club initiation."

Some joke. I didn't think my mom would be all that amused by a parade of vampires or would-be vampires trooping up to our door.

And then I remembered Vennard.

CHAPTER 13

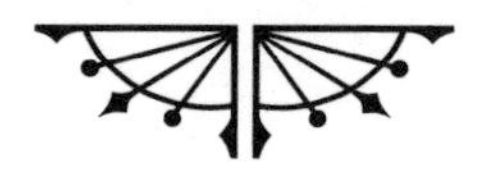

New Orleans: 7:13 P.M. CDT

"Have you seen this? Sigmund brought it." A man in a white turban hands a folded-back newspaper to a woman in a black gown. Two small frown lines like quotation marks dent her brow as she reads. She drops the paper and rushes from the house. The man hurries after her, "Wait, Carlotta, it might be a trap."

Vennard stalks up to the house and pushes the door open. He searches but finds no one. In the foyer he spots the newspaper. He scans the folded-back page, throws his head back and laughs.

Wicklow, West Virginia: 8:21 P.M. EDT

I tried not to think about Vennard. Maybe Eugene had exaggerated his evilness. I didn't mention the ad. No need to upset him. But I did ask him what Vennard would do to him.

"Alors, he will kill me," Eugene said.

"But Eugene, you're a vampire. You can't be killed."

"Oh yes, I can be killed by another vampire, one that is more powerful than I am."

"Why is he more powerful?"

"In the same way that some men are more powerful. And some women. My cousin is evil. He will stop at nothing to get what he wants. Or what he doesn't want. He is the monstre."

I shuddered and shut up. I didn't want to know how one vampire kills another. I just hoped Vennard didn't see the ad. And even if he did, Eugene was probably exaggerating about his powers. People always think that bullies are worse than they really are. Vampires probably think that way, too.

The truce between Bat Ears—I mean—Alison and me had worked so far. She was too busy with the Eugene problem to boss me around. So far. She was bossing Eugene around. In French. It was very peaceful for me. Except that he was always hungry. I caught him sneaking down to the kitchen and had to be stern with him. He would have scared Mom to death.

He wanted milk shakes and ice cream all the time. And he insisted he could fly perfectly well. He didn't need to work out.

"First you said you could barely fly. You were afraid of heights. Then you said you could fly nicely. Now you say you could fly as well as the next vampire."

"Oui. I can. I am just out of the practice."

"I guess it would depend on who the next vampire is," I said. Eugene missed my sarcasm. Or chose to ignore it as he nodded enthusiastically.

"I do not need to pump out."

I agreed with that. He was plenty pumped out. But he still needed to pump up. "Prove it."

His shoulders sagged. He was still a pitiful physical specimen and he knew it. Nobody in 1852 worried about his physical condition or what he ate or exercised beyond a stroll or horseback ride or croquet. Eugene said Henry VIII played tennis in the sixteenth century but look at his physical condition. If Henry had been a vampire, he couldn't have flown. He could hardly walk as a person.

Days went by without any response to the ad. But Alison was optimistic. "Give it time. It's only been a week. We don't know how long it will take on the vampire grapevine."

I was relieved that I hadn't had to explain a bunch of vampires to my mom. I didn't even want to think about what they might be like. Or act like. And what if they were pitiful like Eugene and wanted to move in, too, so I would have to take care of them? My brain reeled with the possibilities. Then there was the Vennard problem.

Bat—Alison told her mother we were working on a project so she could bring over supplies without her mother getting suspicious about the bundles. That helped. But not enough.

Alison rushed over late with Eugene's supper. "We had company," she explained. She'd brought canned tomatoes, two bananas, half a jar of olives, a carton of leftover rice, and half a doughnut.

"Very nutritious," I told her. "A real balanced meal."

"There's grain and fruit and vegetables and protein and carbohydrates," she said.

"Carbohydrates?" I raised my eyebrows.

"The doughnut half."

Eugene ate it plus the pork chop I'd saved from our supper. Then it was exercise time. I slid in the Lydia video. We were all tired of her slippery lavender legs by now.

"Let's take him on a run tonight," Alison suggested.

"Good idea." Eugene was suffering aerobics burnout. This Vennard character was probably off in Transylvania building a vampire amusement park. He would never see the ad in the *Gistville Gazette.*

Eugene went ahead of us on the downhill. The houses were dark, porches empty. The night was quiet except for the frogs and crickets and a dog barking faintly in the distance. The sky was full of bezillions of stars. I had mowed our grass today and the Genneros' and the whole street still smelled fresh as watermelon.

At the foot of the hill we could see stars floating on the Tuscarora. It was that clear here, no smog, few lights. The river flowed silently by as we passed the cemetery.

I felt something on the back of my neck.

"Um, Alison, when you walk by here, do you ever feel something?"

"Like what?"

"Like eyes watching you."

"Dead eyes, you mean?"

"Dead eyes can't watch anything. No, I just sort of feel something." I slapped my neck. "I guess it was a mosquito."

We walked on into the main part of town. Eugene began to beg for a fudge shake.

"Eugene, you just ate," I told him.

"Not dessert."

"What do you think the doughnut was?"

"Carbohydrate," he said innocently.

"Another word for dessert. You're on a diet, remember? So you can get airborne again. Half a doughnut is enough." I was beginning to feel like Eugene's mother.

"But I am much firmer now. Feel." He made a muscle. I didn't want to feel vampire muscle but he insisted. It felt like anybody's muscle only maybe a little flabbier.

Correction.

A lot flabbier. But I didn't want to hurt his feelings. He had been trying. And mostly he had been a good sport about his diet and exercise. He only whined now and then. And he had stopped ordering from Home Shopping. I'd refused a metal detector, a pogo stick, a combination potato peeler-fingernail parer-facial massager, and three sets of matched luggage.

"Please," Eugene begged. "Only one fudge shake."

"No," I said.

"Just one," He turned his pitiful puppy eyes on Alison. "I need protein."

"He had a pork chop," I reminded her.

"That's not much after a century of protein deprivation," she said. She couldn't resist those puppy eyes.

"Wimp." I dug around in my pockets for a few coins. She added some and counted it.

"Okay. One fudge shake coming up," she said. She bought it and Eugene slurped it happily.

"Um, Eugene," I said between slurps. "Where do you think Carlotta is now?" He had seemed unconcerned about her fate. Of course, a century and a half separation could change a person. Even a vampire.

"In Prague, probablement. She was most fond of Prague. We spent the most amusing summer there when we were 201. Or, slurp, was it 202? I cannot remember. Slurp slurp."

Eugene's manners were impeccable but he'd

been watching too much TV. I would have to have a talk with him.

"Don't you want to get in touch with her? Tell her you're um—alive?"

He stopped slurping. "Mais oui. I love Carlotta most of all in the world. But how do I tell her if she is in Prague?"

I started to tell him about directory assistance, but suddenly I had a vision of our next phone bill and trying to explain calls to Prague to Mom. We would have to think of another way. Maybe Alison could make the calls. Her mother was probably accustomed to having calls to Greenland and Queensland and Quatar on their phone bill.

The moon was rising now and with it came a breeze. Moonlight splotched the restless shadows. The back of my neck was feeling queasy again. I know. Only stomachs are supposed to feel that way. Maybe it started in my stomach and spread. All I knew was that something was wrong in Wicklow.

"Let's go back," I said to Alison in a low voice.

"He needs to walk farther," she said.

"Let's go back. He can dance a while with Lydia."

"There's no hurry."

"Listen Bat Ears, I have this feeling . . ."

"DON'T CALL ME THAT."

"Okay, okay." I tried to calm her down but I guess I'd called her that one time too many. I hadn't meant to. It just slipped out.

"I DON'T KNOW WHY YOU EVER CALLED ME THAT. I DON'T HAVE BAT EARS. MY EARS ARE PERFECTLY NORMAL. SEE?" She pulled her hair back to reveal her perfectly normal ears.

"Keep your voice down."

"WHY?"

"Because we don't know what might be listening. Or watching."

I could feel her bristling in the dark, but her concern for Eugene took over. "What kind of feeling?"

"That's just the trouble. I don't know."

"Oh, all right. Turn around, Eugene. Jeff wants to go home."

"Oh, Jeff, you are feeling bad?" Slurp slurp.

"Yes, no. I don't know. Let's just go back."

We retraced our steps. It happened at the cemetery.

Where else?

CHAPTER 14

9:21 P.M. EDT,

Somewhere in the celestial darkness

Carlotta settles herself in the turbulent vapor of a towering cloud. Her thoughts are just as turbulent. The strong headwind would slow her flight tonight. She has already lost precious time. She should have suspected the Cashbeau family. They had always been involved in skulduggery. Singh said Louis had paid them to dispose of Eugene. Louis was clever, but not as clever as he thought he was. Somehow Eugene had escaped. She had been too late in 1852. This time, she must not be. This time Vennard would kill Eugene.

Wicklow, West Virginia: 9:23 P.M. EDT

Something was in the cemetery. Eugene's face was a mask of terror. Light was suddenly sucked away and Wicklow plunged into blackness. A vast whooshing sound like a hurricane-force wind tore across the sky.

Eugene dropped the fudge shake cup. "Run!" he screamed.

Where? The wind seemed all around us. We stood like tombstones, not knowing which way to go. And then a shadow emerged.

"It's Louis, Louis Vennard." Eugene gasped.

The tall, attenuated shadow thrust itself between us and the town. I grabbed Eugene and Alison and pulled them into the cemetery.

Things seemed to claw at us as we entered the city of the dead, things that felt like skeletal hands but were probably only branches. Or imagination. I didn't stop to look. The cemetery was on high ground, far above the highest flood mark, but there were many aboveground tombs like little marble or brick houses. Houses of the dead. The summer night air chilled. I bumped the corner of a tomb and jerked back, as if I'd touched a body.

Our feet crunched on the gravel path. Vennard could track us by sound. I steered them onto soft grass. Our footsteps were silent here but they sounded like drumbeats in my ears. We ran through the tombs, past a marble book, an obelisk, a soldier. We plastered ourselves against a tomb and panted. The marble wall felt like a slab of ice.

"What's going on?" Alison demanded.

"Quiet," I hissed. "It's the evil vampire, the one that wants to kill Eugene. And us too."

"What do you mean?"

"I mean that's another vampire out there."

"Another vampire! That's great. I bet he saw my ad."

Was she dense? "It's not great. It's the worst thing that could happen."

"Why? Who is this vampire? Is he a friend of Eugene's?"

"Keep your voice down." I gave her a quick history.

Even in the dark I could see her eyes roll. "Oh pul-lease, that's ridiculous. Nobody is that evil."

But Eugene had caught his breath enough to gasp out, "It's true, everything that Jeffrey says. Vennard will kill me and make you into vampires forever."

"I guess it's my fault," Alison said.

"It's my fault, too," I said. "I should have told you about Vennard."

"Maybe we can hide inside the tomb," Alison whispered.

Hide inside a tomb?

In the dark?

Was she nuts?

But between Vennard and the tomb I would have to choose the tomb. I tugged at the door.

"Can't. It's locked." I wasn't exactly sorry. The door was solid wood with an ornate lock and carved leaves and acorns, only the acorns were skulls. I glanced up. Marble letters stood out in relief.

Cashbeau. Nothing would get me in that tomb.

"It does not matter," Eugene said. "He knows we are here. We cannot hide from him. Alors, it is useless, truly. He has the most power of all vampires."

"What can we do?" I asked him.

He shrugged. "I do not know. We are doomed."

I was too young to be doomed. I checked around the corner and saw a large marble cross. "Listen, I think we should get behind that cross over there. That should give us some protection."

"It will not," Eugene said, shaking his head mournfully. "Louis likes crosses. He says they tickle him."

"What do you want to do, stay here all night?"

"Moi, I would love that," Eugene said. "But I don't think he will let us."

"What will he do to us?"

He didn't answer. He just shuddered. We joined him.

We didn't have any choice. I wasn't going to let Vennard kill Eugene or turn us into vampires.

"Okay, let's go. Me first, then Eugene, then Alison."

I crouched and ran behind the cross. They followed. We were safe for now. We huddled behind the cross to plan our next move.

Suddenly a loud laugh split the air around us. And a voice deep and sinister slid out of the dark. "Do you really think that little trinket of a cross will protect you?"

"Who are you?" I tried to deepen my voice and sound authoritative like my father in court. "Identify yourself." My voice squeaked on the last word.

He laughed, then said, "Eugene, are you listening?"

Eugene huddled in a pathetic heap next to me.

Vennard's whisper was like a snake in the night.

Eugene whimpered.

"I can't hear you, Eugene."

"Don't answer," I said. Somehow I thought if Eugene spoke, Vennard would gain some kind of power over Eugene and could force him to his will.

"Tell your little friends who I am, Eugene."

Eugene opened his mouth to speak.

"No," I said. "Don't."

"I am Eugene's cousin, Louis Vennard. Tell them, Eugene. Tell them how I tricked you into the trunk."

"We are lost," Eugene moaned.

"Not yet. We'll think of something," I said to keep his spirits up. "We need a plan. Any suggestions?"

"I have one," Alison whispered.

"Let's hear it."

"You get his attention. I'll sneak away and pretend to be a rooster crowing. He'll think it's morning and have to get away from the sun. Then we can escape. Meet me at the marble lamb. Just follow this path beside the cross. It leads to the gate in the alley between the houses on Stephens

Street. It's a shortcut from town. The lamb is in front of the gate. You can't miss it."

So that was how she beat me home all those times. I told her what I thought of her plan. Eugene seconded my opinion.

"Do you have a better one?" she challenged.

I had to admit I didn't.

"Okay, then let's do it. Eugene, are you with us?"

"There is no hope," he moaned.

"That's right, Eugene." The voice sounded closer. "After you fell into my trap at the warehouse, I paid Aristide Cashbeau to remove the trunk and see that it never surfaced again. He did not carry out my wishes. If he were still around I would have to punish him. Unfortunately, he is in the tomb that you so lately left behind you."

My stomach lurched. I gave Alison the sign to go.

"Listen up, Vennard," I said as sternly as I could. My voice sounded funny in my ears, like a record played faster than normal. I tried to sound like Dad in court to divert Vennard's attention while Alison crept away.

"Ur ur urrr ur urhhhhh," Alison crowed nearby.

"Come on." I took Eugene's arm and ran from tomb to tomb straight ahead. My pulse thundered in my ears.

Eugene stumbled. I pulled him up. We were almost there. Our lives depended on speed now as we raced for the statue. A hundred more miles and we were there. Alison met us. I glanced up at the lamb on its pedestal. And then we screamed as one.

Vennard was riding it as though he were on a merry-go-round animal.

We made a U-turn and sped back the way we had come, back to the false safety of the marble cross. I could hear that awful laughter, bouncing off the tomb walls in front of us, behind us, all around us. Stereophonic vampire laughter.

"This is so amusing, Eugene. I did not expect that you would provide such sport. You never did before. You were always so easy to fool, Eugene. Remember the poisoned gingerbread castle? You must have been around ten."

"That was you?"

"Who else?"

"But you poisoned my sweet little chien, Pastille."

"She was a greedy dog. She gobbled the whole thing after I had taken such pains with it, mixing the poison into the icing."

"You, you monstre!" Eugene cried.

"Les monstres have all the fun, Eugene. I am going to have such fun with your little friends."

"You leave them out of this, you dirty rat!"

"Such articulation, Eugene."

"It is all my fault," Eugene moaned, wringing his hands. "I am the cause of your predicament. He wants me. If I go to him, maybe he will let you escape."

"No, Eugene, we can't let you sacrifice yourself for us," Alison said.

"It is the only way. While he is occupied with me, you can make your escape. Perhaps he will forget about you."

"Stay here, Eugene," I said. "It is not your fault any more than it's my fault, or Alison's."

"Non, non, I brought him to you. It is moi he wants. I will decoy him. Then he will gloat and forget about you."

I stared at Eugene. He was going to let Vennard kill him to save us. This chubby, ineffectual vampire was going to be a hero. And I had begrudged having to feed him. "Eugene, if we get out of here alive, I'm going to buy you the biggest fudge shake in the whole state of West Virginia."

"Non, non, my friend, I will buy you one. Non, I will buy you bananas Foster in New Orleans. And cherries jubilee."

"This is not the time to discuss food," Alison said.

"Alas," Eugene said, "farewell, my friends."

Things seemed to go into slow motion here, and I guess it was a good thing because it gave me time to act. Eugene took a step forward, to sacrifice himself for us.

I grabbed his shirt and pulled him back. "No, Eugene, we can't let you do it." But he was stronger after all that pumping up and feeding. He kept going and I was left holding air.

I made a flying tackle and brought him down. Alison and I dragged him back to temporary safety.

"Non, non, my friends. You must not do this. It is your only chance for the escape."

"We won't let him have you," Alison said.

"We'll think of something else," I told him.

Vennard laughed. It sounded the way slivers of glass would feel going through skin.

"This is so entertaining. I almost hate to end it. But there is no escape. It is too late, Eugene. If I do not get them tonight, there is tomorrow night. They will be mine now for eternity. But first, the unfinished business of Eugene."

Eugene put his head in his hands. "What can we do?"

I had a feeble suggestion. "If we can hold him off until the sun comes up for real, maybe then we can escape."

Eugene shook his head. "That is an old myth," he said between his fingers. "The dawn will not save us. Vampires don't like it, but it will not stop Louis. He is too evil. The normal vampire rules do not, how do you say, camp his style."

"Cramp." So much for that theory.

The marble tombs gleamed in the moonlight. The cemetery was as bright as downtown Wicklow as I cast about for a glimmer of hope. Then the light dimmed. I looked up to find the reason and saw a cloud approaching the moon. Maybe this was the chance we needed.

"Listen up, guys. I have another plan. There's a cloud coming. I think we should try to slip around Vennard on the riverside while the moon is behind the cloud. Then we can go up Stephens

Street. He's expecting us to try the shortcut again through the cemetery to the lamb."

"It will not work, Jeffrey," Eugene said.

"Don't be negative," Alison said. "Even vampire eyes need light. It's the only plan we have."

"We have to try it," I said.

"It will not work. It is true he needs light but not as much as mortals to see. We cannot run from him. He is a vampire. He can fly, remember?"

"Yeah, right. I almost forgot."

"I know, you think I am a failure as a vampire. But my heart was never in it."

"It's okay, Eugene," I said. "Don't worry about that."

"It is no use," he said again. "We cannot escape him. I know this."

But he got to his feet as we waited for the cloud to reach the moon. When it did, the cemetery darkened into a maze of murky shadows.

"Now," I whispered.

We slipped around the corner of the cross. The cemetery was as silent as—well, a grave. We slid behind the next tomb and felt our way along its walls. We made our way from tomb to cross to tomb to monument to urn to obelisk, and even a marble boat until we reached the last tomb.

I led the way. The gate was straight ahead. We were going to make it. But the cloud passed by the moon and its light flowed over the cemetery. We came face-to-face with the visage chiseled from ice, obsidian eyes glittering like a cobra's.

"Good evening," Louis Vennard said.

CHAPTER 15

Wicklow, West Virginia: 10:03 P.M. EDT

We screamed. In unison.

I admit it wasn't cool.

In fact it was very uncool. But we weren't into being cool right then. We were scared to death.

His face was awful. Evil shone from his eyes like black holes of death against the white of his face. Fangs gleamed in the red cave of his mouth, fangs for a rattlesnake to die for. Out of the cave came that horrible laughter, and I knew that everything Eugene had told us about himself, Vennard, and Carlotta was absolutely true.

The laughter seemed to go on for a couple of hours but it was probably only a few seconds.

We watched helplessly as he raised his arms to strike.

The cloud came back suddenly and darkness descended like a cloak.

"Run!" I yelled.

Wind whooshed behind us. We held hands and raced through the cemetery gates.

"We can't make it up the hill in time," Alison said.

"No, we'll go out River Street and find a place to hide," I panted.

We ran along the road beside the river, around a bend and then another bend. Eugene tripped but we held on to him and he didn't fall.

"We can't go on running," Alison said. "Eugene has had it. We've got to stop."

I noticed that Alison was panting, too, as my own breath wheezed in my ears.

"Where?"

"I don't know. Maybe there's someplace along the river. Maybe we can get in the water and breathe through reeds until he gives up and goes home."

I didn't want to get in that dark river and be a snake snack, but I didn't want to be a vampire snack either.

Eugene muttered something between pants and wheezes.

"I know, I know. Vennard can probably see underwater," I said.

The river shone in the moonlight. I started to panic. I clamped my teeth together and tried to shut out the picture of Louis Vennard, soaring above us, cape outspread, fangs flashing in the moonlight as he swooped down for the kill.

Around another bend I saw something dark against the bank. It looked like an old boat. "We can hide here. P-P-Permission to come aboard," my teeth chattered to any ghost of a captain that might be hanging around.

The boat was old and decrepit and resembled a tugboat. We would probably crash through rotten boards and break our legs. Something caught my ankle. A snake? I kicked at it and would have fallen overboard if Alison and Eugene hadn't been holding on to me.

"It is only a rope," Eugene said.

"Quick, we have to go below before Vennard sees us." We inched our way across the deck. I bumped into the cabin. We found steps. There was no way but down.

We scrambled down the narrow stairs into the

cabin filled with boards and debris and no telling what else.

Or who.

"Quiet!" Alison ordered.

Footsteps sounded on the deck overhead. We squeezed ourselves into a corner and tried not to pant.

Our lungs were not in the best working order. Especially Eugene's.

The footsteps moved along the deck, to the steps. The first one creaked.

"Eugene? Where are you, Eugene?" The whispery voice seemed to search the wooden walls, the piles of debris, then lingered where it encountered us.

We were caught. I wondered what my mother would think. Could I be prosecuted for being a vampire? Would my dad represent me in court? My son, the vampire, he could introduce me to all his and Moira's new friends. I perked up momentarily. Moira would hate having a vampire for a stepson.

"Eugene?" The whisper was close now.

I could feel myself sweating.

Correction.

I could feel myself drowning in sweat.

"Eugene?"

The whisper was almost on top of us.

"Eugene, my dear. It is me, Carlotta."

"Carlotta? Dear, dear, dear Carlotta!" Eugene leaped up and there were kissy sounds in the air above us.

Alison and I stood up. We weren't going to be vampirized right away. We were still holding hands. I didn't let go.

Neither did she.

At last we were meeting the vampire Carlotta. And it was too dark to see. Eugene introduced us. In French. They chattered away. Alison contributed sometimes. Now and then she took time out to tell me what was going on.

"He is explaining everything that has happened to him since 1852."

"Great. And is she doing the same thing?"

"No, she just told him that she has eluded Vennard since the night Eugene disappeared and has been searching everywhere for him. She never suspected the Cashbeau family."

"Great. May I remind you bilingual people—and by the way, I do a mean Spanish—that we are expecting company at any minute and we'd better have a plan."

Eugene said something in French and they all laughed. "He said that you are big on plans," Alison translated, "and some of them even work."

Ha ha.

"Well, I'm all out of plans today and not expecting a shipment anytime soon."

"It is all right, Jeffrey," Carlotta said. "I have a plan. But you are right, we must hurry and implement the plan. I made a cloud and then tricked Louis to give you time to escape from the cemetery."

"You made a cloud. How did you do that?"

"I flew under the moon and waved my arms. It is simple, non? But then Louis saw it was I. Louis is terribly vain. I told him I had eluded him because it was a game, like chess. And he had just put the queen in check. To the victor goes the prize. But I was tired from the long trip and needed to freshen up by biting the girl."

Alison suddenly stiffened and so did I. We must have made some kind of sound in the dark because Carlotta quickly said, "Non, non, do not worry. I am like Eugene. We do not bite people. But Louis doesn't know that. I told him that with strength from the girl, I would help him catch the other two and we could have some sport. But in a minute or two he will realize that I have tricked him and he will be very dangerous then."

I thought Vennard was very dangerous all the time but I kept quiet. The ball was in the vampire court.

"What can we do?" Eugene asked.

"This boat is a trap," Alison said. "There's no way out except the way you came in."

"And if we go back on the road, Vennard will find us," I said.

"Indeed, you are both right. But my plan will work. Eugene, take off your clothes," Carlotta ordered.

"Pardon?" Eugene sputtered.

"Not all of them. Just your shirt. Do not be modest now, Eugene." She rummaged around in the dark, banging things around, making so much noise that Vennard would have no doubts where we were. I hoped she knew what she was doing.

When a little moonlight seeped in through holes in the boat, I saw a beautiful woman with pale skin and black hair hanging something that looked like my dad's shirt in a wooden locker.

"Ah, that is better. When Louis looks in the closet, he will see the shirt and think it is Eugene. We will have only an instant to slam the door on him. Now we must hide. Pile up those boards and get behind them. He will be here soon."

We made a sort of barricade in the corner and had just enough time to crouch behind it before there was a thud on the deck above us. I thought it was a pitiful plan. But it was a plan.

And it was the only plan in town.

CHAPTER 16

Wicklow, West Virginia: 10:17 P.M. EDT

I turned my wrist over so the luminous digits on my watch wouldn't show in the dark. The moon was behind a cloud again. It didn't matter. I was sure Vennard could see right through the deck into the dark of the cabin.

Vennard's footsteps followed the route Carlotta had taken, across the deck, down the stairs.

"I know you are in here. I can smell you, Eugene. You always smelled like stale bread."

He wasn't such a smart vampire. Eugene didn't smell like stale bread. Tonight he smelled like Groovy, the aftershave Moira gave me last Christmas. Then I realized he was just taunting

Eugene so he would reveal our hiding place. I hoped Eugene wouldn't fall for it.

"I can smell you, Eugene. I'm getting closer. You're in that locker, aren't you? You always liked to hide in closets, even when you were a small boy. It always amused me to pretend not to find you. I was free from your tiresomeness for days."

I thought about the little boy Eugene hiding for days in a closet, thinking he had fooled Vennard.

Pitiful.

The footsteps came closer. I concentrated on what we had to do. It was such a simple plan. A flimsy plan. A—you get the picture.

I didn't want to think about what would happen if the plan didn't work.

Suddenly Vennard was in front of the locker.

"Come out, Eugene, wherever you are!" He sent his laughter after us like some kind of vampire weapon, flying all around in the tiny cramped boat cabin, searching for us. Like a bat.

Vennard opened the locker. Without a sound, Eugene and Carlotta leaped out and gave him a mighty shove. He pitched headfirst into the locker. Alison and I slammed the door behind him. I rammed a length of iron pipe through the handle. Then we piled all the debris we could find in front of the locker door and jammed boards between the door and the wall of the boat. I hoped that would hold him.

Vennard pounded on the door, snarling and roaring and threatening us.

"Now it's your turn to be locked up, Vennard," I said. "See how you like it."

"Take that, you dirty rat!" Eugene said in his best James Cagney imitation, which, to tell you the truth, wasn't bad.

"Let's get out of here!" We scrambled up the stairs and back to dry land. The night seemed to have settled down into a regular night. The moonlight didn't seem sinister now, just bright. We walked up Stephens Street to my house.

I was shocked to see that it wasn't even time for Mom to come home yet. I was glad that I wouldn't have to tell her I was a vampire. Although I wouldn't have minded so much telling Moira.

Carlotta was beautiful and elegant with sparkly green eyes and shiny black hair. She wore a long black cape over a floaty black-sequined gown.

We were all starving and if this had been anywhere but Wicklow, West Virginia, we could have ordered out for pizza. Well, almost anywhere. I know there are other places in the world that don't deliver pizzas at night. The Frizzeria was closed now. Eugene would have to wait for his giant fudge shake. But we had frozen pizzas we fixed up and popcorn and sodas. You wouldn't believe how hungry fighting off an evil vampire can make you.

"But Carlotta, chère, how did you find me?" Eugene asked as he ate a bowl of popcorn. He was wrapped in my bedspread togalike and looked more Roman than vampire.

"I read the ad in the *Gistville Gazette.*"

"Ad?" Eugene's face was blank.

"Mais oui. Did you not place an ad in the newspaper?"

"I put it in," Alison said. "We thought Eugene was lonely for, you know, company like yourself." Her voice trailed off as Eugene stared at her in surprise. "We thought you'd be happier with other vampires."

"I was very happy here with just you and Jeff, but I am even happier that Carlotta has found me. I did not know she was searching for me."

"How did you get the *Gazette*?" I asked.

"A friend showed it to me. We have a sort of grapevine. That is how Vennard found out as well, the ad."

"You mean there are vampires around here? Besides Eugene?" I said.

"Around," Carlotta said vaguely. "They mostly live secluded lives. They don't actually bite people. Vennard and his kind live in cities where they will not attract attention. Only the evil ones cause trouble. Just like non-vampires."

"I'm glad to hear it," I said. Alison and I looked at each other. We were thinking the same thing. Now we would go around suspicious of everybody at night.

"It is time for us to go, Eugene, my dear," Carlotta said. "Do you want to dress for the trip? I do not think you can fly very well in a bedspread."

Eugene went back upstairs. Wait until she found out he couldn't fly at all. I threw stuff into the dishwasher and wiped off the table.

Eugene didn't come down right away. Then he peeked around the stairway. "Pssst, Jeffrey, can you come here? Jeffrey, I cannot let Carlotta see me in this suit."

"You have to, Eugene." All my ideas were used up.

He looked ready to cry, but he couldn't fit into my clothes. Slowly, he went into the kitchen. His shrunken suit looked ridiculous with sleeves to his elbows, trousers to his knees.

"Oh, Eugene, you look adorable. Like Little Lord Fauntleroy!" Carlotta exclaimed. "But what happened to your suit?"

"Um, I washed it in the washer and dried it in the dryer. I guess it sort of, well, shrank," I said.

"No matter. If we meet anybody in flight I'll explain that we are on the way to a costume party."

I didn't want to think about who or what they might meet in flight.

Carlotta smoothed her hair to make her more hairodynamic, no doubt. Eugene was swooning over being called adorable. I couldn't tell her there wasn't going to be any flight. Not from Eugene anyway.

But I didn't have to.

"Carlotta, dear," he said uncomfortably, "I am afraid I cannot make the flight with you."

"What do you mean? After being apart all these years, you do not want to be with me now?"

"No, no," he said. "It is not that."

"Is there someone else? Eugene, were you alone in that trunk?"

"Yes, he was," I said. "I can guarantee that."

"There is no one else, Carlotta, chère. It is," he hung his head, "it is that I cannot fly. I lost the ability locked in that trunk all those years."

"Is that all?"

He nodded without looking at her.

"Nonsense," she said briskly. "Vampires of all persuasions can fly. All you have to do is try."

He shook his head. "No, I cannot. I have tried."

"Eugene, look at me."

First, he raised his head, then his eyes.

"Do you want to return with me to New Orleans?"

"Oui, Carlotta. With all my heart."

"Then you will. All you have to do is try. Come, Jeffrey, Alison. We will help Eugene fly. Let us go outside."

She gave us instructions on how to help a vampire fly. I hoped this worked. I found a faded striped beach towel and she pinned it to his shoulders.

"It isn't exactly a cape, but it will have to do," she said.

We trooped out the front door. Wicklow was quiet and most of the houses were dark.

"It is good that we are high on this hill," Carlotta said. "We will pick up air currents here. Are you ready, Eugene my dear?"

He looked at me and gulped.

I stuck out my hand. "I'm going to miss you, Eugene." And suddenly I realized I really was. Eugene took my hand and I pumped his furiously. His eyes were getting moist.

"Jeffrey, my friend." He seized my shoulders and before I could stop him, he kissed me on both cheeks—right, then left.

"Hey," I protested the way I did when Mom kissed me in public.

"It is the French way," he said. He let me go and kissed Alison's cheeks.

Then Carlotta kissed me twice also. I decided I liked French ways.

Carlotta kissed Alison's cheeks. "Now we must go," she said.

We stood at the top of Stephens Street. Carlotta took one of Eugene's hands, Alison the other. They ran with him while I ran behind, ready to help his feet into the air at the first sign of liftoff.

We ran, he lifted, I raised his feet, he landed on his nose.

This was not going to be easy.

We started over. We ran, Eugene seemed to lift a little, I raised his feet, and he crashed again.

After the sixth attempt we were all huffing and

puffing. Our pounding feet sounded like a herd of buffalo. The neighbors would soon be out with shotguns to bag their limit.

We stopped to rest. Eugene was desolate.

"It is no use," he said over and over. "I've lost it."

I kept one ear tuned for Mom's car. I could hear the conversation.

"What are you doing now, Jeffrey?"

"I'm helping this vampire get off the ground, Mom. He has to fly to New Orleans before dawn."

Oh, man.

Mom! I thought of her pep talks. That was what Eugene needed.

"Eugene, listen to me, you can do anything if you just try. That's all it takes. Just a little effort on your part. You will be amazed at how far a little effort will take you." I went on and on like that until I thought Alison was going to bop me. I wound it up. "Now let me see you try."

"I don't know," Eugene began.

I was desperate and out of desperation comes inspiration. So Mom says.

"Eugene, think of your heroes. Think of Lindbergh flying the Atlantic. He did it and so can you."

"But, Jeffrey, he had a plane."

"A mere detail," I scoffed. "He was all alone. You are not. You have us to help you and Carlotta to fly with you. So you are even luckier than Lindbergh."

"Mais non. Lindbergh had a plane."

"Okay," I said. "Think of your other idols and heroes. Think of Tarzan, think of Mary Poppins, think of Fred Flintstone." I don't think Fred ever flew, but I was getting inspired as I tried to remember all those old movies and cartoons. "Think of John Wayne. He wouldn't let a little detail like not having a plane stop him from flying. Think of Superman and Spiderman and George of the Jungle."

"Wiley Coyote!" Eugene contributed. "Gilligan!"

"Well, yes." I didn't want to discourage him. "Think of Harrison Ford and Clark Gable. Eugene, THINK OF JIMMY STEWART!"

"Jimmy Stewart!" Eugene's face brightened and I knew I had said the magic words.

"Just keep saying over and over to yourself, Jimmy Stewart, Jimmy Stewart, Jimmy Stewart."

We got into position. They began to run just as a car's lights flashed at the foot of the street.

Eugene quickly achieved liftoff and I thought he would make it this time. I lifted his feet. I could hear him chanting under his breath, "Jimmystew-artjimmystewartjimmystewartjimmystewart."

Alison let go of his hand as Carlotta and Eugene were airborne. They flew over our heads and swooped around in a loop, heading south to New Orleans.

And not a minute too soon. Mom's headlights picked Alison and me out of the dark.

"Jeff, what are you two doing out here?"

"Um, just checking out the moon, Mom. Isn't it a great night?"

"Well, watch out for bats."

"Bats won't bother you. Bats are nothing. It's vampires you have to watch out for."

"Oh, Jeffrey, you and your imagination!" But she was smiling. She was probably glad to see me with Alison.

And surprised.

CHAPTER 17

New Orleans: 5:12 A.M. CDT

Eugene and Carlotta arrive at his house in the Garden District. She unlocks the wrought iron door. "I have kept it ready for you all these years. It is all just as you left it. I didn't change a thing except to have a few modern conveniences added, like electricity and air-conditioning and central heat."

"Well then, we have to buy a car," Eugene says. "A sports car. We'll be just like Steed and Mrs. Peel on *The Avengers.* Oh, I've learned so much from TV. There are so many new things now. Did you know they have these wonderful vacuum cleaners and foam cutters and . . ."

Wicklow, West Virginia: 9:28 A.M. EDT

I went over to Alison's and knocked on the front door. "Oh, hello, Jeff," Mrs. Gennero said. She was wearing a smock smeared with paint. Her nose had a green streak. "Alison has been expecting you. I saved you a stack of blueberry pancakes."

I could never turn down homemade pancakes. Or any kind of pancakes. If Mrs. Gennero was trying to lure me over to her house, she was going about it in the right way. It wasn't so bad over here. The kitchen was huge and had rocking chairs in front of a fireplace, a tricycle under the table, plants in the windows, and old games on the walls. Maybe I would come over sometimes.

When Mom wasn't home.

Just to have somewhere to go.

Alison sat and watched me eat.

"Do you realize what a unique experience we have just had?" she asked.

"Are you going to write about it for the paper?" I finished my glass of milk. "Or sell it to the tabloids?"

"You have a milk mustache. No. Who would believe it unless it was a fiction book? We don't have any proof."

Technically we did have proof. We had Vennard.

"There's nothing wrong with writing it as fiction."

"Terrific idea." She grinned. I began to wonder if I had thought of it entirely by myself.

"We can use my computer," she said. "I bet we can finish it before school starts."

"Do you think anybody will publish it? I mean, because we're kids?"

"We won't tell them." Alison was resourceful. I'll give her that. "I bet we can get extra credit in English."

Dad would be surprised. Mom, too. Moira could introduce me to all her friends—my stepson, the writer.

But before we could start on the book, we had one other job to do. We got her father's tools and went down to the river.

I was jumpy about going back on the boat, but we had to nail the boards down so that Vennard couldn't ever get out. But when we rounded the bend the boat was gone.

"It has to be here," Alison said. "It has to."

"It could have sunk or something," I offered. "It was pretty beat up."

"It was wedged against the bottom."

"Maybe it got blown out into the river."

"There was no storm last night. A boat can't just disappear."

But this one had. We searched down the river, along the shallows. No trace. The boat was gone and Vennard with it.

"We'd better let Carlotta and Eugene know," Alison said. "I'll write them a letter. They probably don't have fax or E-mail."

Eugene on the Internet. I didn't even want to think about it.

"Then we can start on the book," Alison said.

"We're never going to be safe from Vennard," I said.

"Oh, stop worrying," she said. "He's at the bottom of the Tuscarora somewhere. We're perfectly safe."

"I don't think vampires can drown," I said as we started up Stephens Street.

"That's a great ending," Alison said. "We'll use it."

ORLAND PARK
PUBLIC LIBRARY
A Natural Connection